GRIZZ
THE CHAOS DEMONS MC
BOOK 2

NICOLA JANE

GRIZZ
The Chaos Demons MC
By
Nicola Jane

This book is a work of fiction. The names, characters, places, and incidents are all products of the author's imagination and are not to be construed as real. Any similarities are entirely coincidental.

GRIZZ Copyright © 2024 by Nicola Jane. All rights are reserved. No part of this
book may be used or reproduced in any manner without written permission from the author,
except in the case of brief quotations used in articles or reviews. For information, contact Nicola Jane.

Cover Designer: Wingfield Designs
Editor: Rebecca Vazquez, Dark Syde Books
Proofreader: Jackie Ziegler, Dark Syde Books
Formatting: V.R Formatting

Spelling Note

Please note, this author resides in the United Kingdom and is using British English. Therefore, some words may be viewed as incorrect or spelled incorrectly, however, they are not.

Trigger Warning

This book contains triggers for violence, explicit scenes, and some dirty talking bikers. If any of this offends you, put your concerns in writing to Axel, the club's President, and he'll get back to you . . . maybe.

Acknowledgments

Thank you to all my wonderful readers, and anyone else that supports me—you rock!

Playlist

What Would You Do? – City High
Most Girls – Pink
I'm N Luv (Wit a Stripper) – T-Pain ft. Mike Jones
Unpretty – TLC
Stole – Kelly Rowland
What Was I Made For? – Billie Eilish
The Voice Within – Christina Aguilera
A Little Too Much – Shawn Mendes
Try Sleeping with a Broken Heart – Alicia Keys
When The Sun Goes Down – Arctic Monkeys
i tried - Camylio
Train Wreck – James Arthur
the reason i hate home - Munn
Boys Like You – Anna Clendening
Falling – Harry Styles
the boy is mine – Ariana Grande
if u think i'm pretty – Artemas

CHAPTER 1

GRIZZ

I scrub my calloused hands over my tired face and focus my eyes on Axel as he goes over last week's figures. "So, that about wraps it up," he says, running his fingers over the gavel. "Actually, one last thing." I inwardly groan. I've got shit loads to do today, and we've been in church an hour already. "Lex made a suggestion," he begins, and the brothers start to shift in their seats.

We all love the Pres's old lady, but she's been making way too many suggestions lately, from separating our recycling to holding bonding nights. "Just hear me out," he adds, sensing our protests before he's even spoken.

"Pres, no disrespect, but Lexi's last suggestion ended in Duke and Cash wearing face masks. Fucking face masks," says Smoke, and a few of us snigger.

"It was a damn pamper night," snaps Duke. "It's what we were meant to do."

Axel holds up his hands, and we fall silent again. "This is actually a good idea. Each of you will be assigned a club girl to watch over," he begins and groans erupt. "Look, Lex's got a point. It's a good way to keep an eye on everyone."

"What are we keeping an eye on the whores for?" asks Duke.

"Because they're people too," says Axel, shifting uncomfortably.

"Jesus, you need to get Lexi pregnant or find her a new fucking job," I mutter, standing. "We got better things to do than have pamper nights and watching the club whores."

Axel squares his shoulders. "Sit the fuck down, I haven't finished." I roll my eyes and flop back down in my chair. I might be pissed at his recent efforts to please Lexi, but I won't show him disrespect. "If we're watching them closely, they can't be sneaking off and giving information to our enemies, and fuck knows we got a lot of those lately. Not only that, but we don't know much about them, and if they're hanging around in our club, we should know everything."

"We know they're good at fucking and sucking, Pres. I ain't interested in much else," says Shadow.

"This club needs to feel more like a family," snaps Axel. "It don't feel like it did when I was growing up around here. So, you'll each be assigned to a woman and you'll do as I fucking say."

"And what exactly do we have to do?" I ask. "Because they're gonna think they're in line to becoming our old ladies the second we start showing an interest."

"We'll discuss it tomorrow in church," says Axel, slamming the gavel on the table to dismiss us. Before I can exit, he calls me back, and once everyone else has left, he sits back in his chair. "So, you wanna tell me what's going on?"

I tap my fingers impatiently on the large oak table. "Nothing."

"Now, I feel like you're trying to piss me off."

"I just don't get you," I snap. "You're the President, but every goddamn meeting ends with an idea from Lexi."

"Why's that a problem?" In truth, I don't know why it pisses me off, so I shrug. "You jealous?" he asks, smirking.

I sigh heavily. "I just don't want to sit with my brothers and put on a fucking face mask," I mutter. "I don't want to keep an eye on the whores."

He sits forward, looking me in the eye. "Brother, I'll be honest, I don't want to do that shit either, but when you get yourself an old lady—"

"I won't," I cut in.

He sighs before continuing. "When you get yourself an old lady, you'll realise you do whatever you can to make them happy."

"Well, I won't be wearing face masks," I mutter.

"I just need her to feel . . . welcome. She's trying to find her place in this club, and when there are hardly any old ladies here to keep her busy, it's my job."

"Make some brothers take an old lady then, keep her busy."

He grins. "Are you offering yourself up as tribute?"

"Fuck if I am," I mutter, pushing to stand and heading for the door. "I've got shit to do. Don't bother me with any more bullshit from Lexi," I say as I pull open the door to find Lexi waiting. She arches a brow. "Lexi," I mutter, nodding in greeting.

"I take it you told him?" she asks Axel, and I stop to listen.

Axel smirks. "Not yet."

"Now what?" I ask.

"It can wait until tomorrow. Go finish your bar."

The new bar is my pride and joy. It's a micro-pub with traditional furnishings and fittings I've restored myself. The club will use it to clean money, but out of all the businesses we have, it's my favourite. I've poured my heart and soul into it.

I place the last screw in the sign and climb down the ladder, stepping back to take it in. "The Bar," comes a voice from behind me. I turn, smiling at the sight of my neighbour, Danii. She runs the coffee shop next door to the bar, and while I've been working my arse off the last few weeks, she's been supplying me with coffee and bacon rolls. "It finally has a name," she adds.

"Perfect, right?"

She grins. "I guess so. I mean, we've been calling it that all along."

"Exactly."

"Coffee?" she asks. I give a nod and follow her into her shop. It's pink and girly inside, but as she explained when we first met, she wanted to make it hers, so she put her personality into it.

I take a seat and watch as she makes my coffee. If I was looking for the perfect woman for the back of my bike, she'd be it. She's gorgeous, with the body of a goddess. "Have you got a date for the opening yet?" she asks, turning and catching me looking at her backside. I sit back, and she smirks, placing the coffee down for me. "Cake?" she asks, lifting the lid on a fresh sponge. I give a nod cos she makes insanely good cake.

"A couple weeks, I reckon," I reply. "Almost done inside, and then I gotta have the pumps installed. My President needs to give the go-ahead and then I'm good to go."

"President," she repeats. "That's Axel, right?" I give a nod, and she returns a satisfied smile. "See, I'm getting good at remembering this stuff. Is he still loved up with . . . Lexi?" I nod again, and she fist pumps the air.

"A little too loved up if you ask me."

"Oh god, don't be one of those jealous best friends," she says, groaning dramatically.

I arch a brow. "I'm not jealous. I'm happy for him. Lexi is everything he needs, but she's got some crazy ideas and he jumps on them to impress her. Fuck, she had us listening to waterfalls and shit to try and relax."

Danii laughs. "Meditation?"

"Right, that's what she called it. You ever been in a room full of bikers listening to waterfalls?" I ask, and she shakes her head, still laughing. "It's not normal."

"I've never been in a room full of bikers full stop," she says. "I imagine it's a little intimidating."

"We're pussycats," I say with a wink. "Maybe you can come by one evening," I add, staring down at my coffee. "See for yourself." When I look up again, she's biting on her lower lip in that way she does when she's trying hard not to smile. "I mean, if you want."

"I'd like that. I'd like that a lot."

I take a bite of the cake, closing my eyes in appreciation. "Bring a cake. The guys will love you forever."

The following morning in church, Axel unfolds a piece of paper and clears his throat. "Okay, so yesterday, I told you about watching the club girls. Well, I've made up a list of who I'll be pairing you up with."

"Not this bullshit again," I mutter. "Pres, I don't have time to babysit, and what the fuck are we gonna do when they're working or with another brother? Are we meant to watch?"

Axel shrugs. "I don't know. I haven't thought about it."

He begins reeling off his list, and when I don't hear my name right away, I know I'm in for some more bad news. When he finally says my name, I groan, burying my head in my hands.

"Don't say it," I hiss. "Out of all the girls, you give me the hardest one?"

"Man, she's easy," says Cash. "She don't fucking talk. I'll swap her for London. That girl's got a mouth bigger than the city she was named after."

"No one's swapping," snaps Axel. "I thought long and hard, and Fable needs someone with patience." A few sniggers erupt and I glare at the men until they quiet down. "The rest of you fuckers get out," Axel demands. "Let me talk to my VP." Once they've gone, I fix him with an unimpressed glare. "The reason I paired you with Fable," he begins, "is because I suspect her the most."

"Of?"

"Talking to the police."

I frown. "You suspect the fucking mute is talking to the police?" We have our own inside man, and even though Lexi is no longer working undercover for the force, they're still getting information on us.

"She's a select mute, meaning she picks and chooses when she talks."

"And I can tell you now, she isn't gonna talk to me, Pres."

"I chose you because I know you'll get her talking, brother. Women can't resist that cheeky chappie shit you've got going on." He slides a piece of paper towards me. "These are the shifts she's putting in at Zen this week. Maybe walk her home or something, find out where she's been hiding."

"Great, thanks," I say, sarcasm dripping from my voice. "Is there any other reason you think she's the grass, other than she doesn't speak?"

"She hasn't been staying in her room at the clubhouse."

"So? The women aren't obligated to."

"Where else is she staying, though? She's too mysterious for my liking, Grizz. I'm trusting my gut on this one."

"If you're so certain it's her, why are all the other brothers paired up with a whore?"

"I can't single her out, she'd be suspicious," he says with a grin. "Now, go and do some fucking work."

LUNA

I gently lay Ivy in her Moses basket right as there's a loud banging on the door. I groan when she jumps, opening her eyes. "Fuck," I whisper before cringing. "Sorry," I add, picking her up. My daughter might only be a few weeks old, but I've vowed to stop the bad language.

I pull the door open, and my older brother, Nathaniel, pushes past me, followed by two of his meathead friends. My heart immediately slams faster in my chest. Since having Ivy, he's been easier on me, but I'm expecting it to return to normal any day now.

I follow them into the kitchen, holding Ivy close to my chest, and watch as Nate raids my fridge. "Got any beer?" he asks, piling meat and cheese into his hand.

"No, you know I don't keep that stuff in the flat," I say.

He opens the ham I was going to treat myself to later and eats it right from the pack. "Start buying it," he says between mouthfuls, "for when I come round." I give a nod, even though I have no intention of doing so. Stocking my fridge with beer and too much junk food will result in him calling around a lot more, despite him having a room at Mum's flat, which is just a floor above mine.

I hate his visits, but mostly, I hate him. He's just like my dad—a no good, waste of space who loves himself so much, he finds it impossible to think anyone could find him a repulsive piece of crap. And on top of that, he uses threats and violence to keep me and Mum in check. *He really is just like my dad.* "You working later?" he asks.

"Yeah." There's no point lying. If he finds out, he'll make my life more of a living hell.

He slaps his mate on the back and gives him a grin, "See, told yah." He then looks in my direction again. "Danny here is gonna come over. See him right, would yah?"

"Clients have to book in," I say, shaking my head. "I can't just take walk-ins."

"Then book him in," he says, fixing me with a glare that tells me he'll lose his shit if I dare to push this. But since Thalia took over at The Zen Den, it's impossible for us to run our own client list.

"And all payments have to be made at the front desk," I add. "I can't do freebies anymore."

Nathaniel moves fast until he's in my face and I'm pressed against the wall. On pure instinct, I shield Ivy. "Then you better help him out now. Put the fucking brat down and get in the bedroom."

"Nate," I whisper, hating how my tone is pleading.

His mobile rings and he steps back, allowing me to breathe a sigh of relief. "What?" he barks into the handset. "On my way." He gives a nod to his friends and they file out. He gives me one last sneering look before following them.

I release a long, shaky breath and rush to lock the door. I really need to move out of this area to somewhere my family can't find me.

―――

I've been off work for the last eight weeks. This is my first night back since having Ivy just two weeks ago, and although I know it's probably way too early to be having sex, Thalia has promised to give me an easy shift.

And so far, my evening has run smoothly, which is rare when you work in a brothel. *Trust me.*

By midnight, it's quieting down and I've just said goodnight to my fourth caller. I sit in the shared living room and relax back, praying my shift will end at one a.m. like it's supposed to. Thalia saunters over. "You heard what Axel's put in place?" she asks, filing her pointy nails. I shake my head. Since I found out I was pregnant at six months gone, I've spent less and less time at the clubhouse. "He's putting his guys on you ladies." I frown. "Apparently, it's all part of a new scheme that little miss perfect came up with. She wants the club to feel more like a 'family'," she says, rolling her eyes and using air quotes.

The bell rings out on the front desk and she rolls her eyes for a second time then goes to attend to the caller. A minute later, she appears with Mr. Green. I give her my best desperate look, but it's obvious I'm going to have to take the smelly fucker because there's no one else around. "Fable is free, Mr. Green," Thalia says sweetly, and I know she wants to gag because his bad body odour is already filling up the small space.

"Actually, she isn't," comes a voice from the reception area. A second later Grizz, the Vice President from The Chaos Demons, appears. "I booked her."

I give Thalia a smug smile and stand. "There's nothing in the books," she snaps. "How many times do I have to nag Axel to remind you bikers that you have to book a slot the same as everyone else?"

Grizz ignores her and grabs my hand, leading me up the stairs to my room. Once inside, I offer a smile, because in front of these guys, I never speak. A doctor diagnosed me as a selective mute when I was fourteen. I'd stopped speaking back in school after being horribly bullied. I was facing all kinds of trauma at home and having no break from it in school was the final straw.

I find it much easier to talk to people these days, especially once I know them, but I do it for the mystery with these guys. They like that I don't talk. It also makes me popular amongst the club, although I've only ever slept with Grizz once, when he came out of prison.

I remove my silk robe, letting it pool to the floor. Grizz shakes his head. "I came to take you home, sweetheart, not fuck. Get dressed." I frown, so he continues, "I'm your new babysitter. Pres wants us to watch you ladies." I shake my head. I don't need a babysitter, and I certainly don't need a biker poking around in my already messy life. I haven't even told anyone about Ivy. "I can't take you home at one when you finish your shift, so I'll pay for an hour and get you home early, how's that?" Weird that he wants to pay me but not have sex. I shrug, and he hands me a roll of cash. "Get dressed," he repeats, turning his back and looking out the window.

Grizz had no idea where I lived, so I had to write down my address. The rundown, three-story apartments were built back in the sixties and haven't had work done to them since. They're practically falling down, but since having Ivy, I've had no choice but to stay here instead of the club. I get off the bike and hand the helmet back to Grizz. He stores it away then removes his own. "I'll come up," he says, also getting off the bike.

"No," I say quickly, and his eyes widen at hearing my voice.

A smirk pulls at his lips. "Yes, Fable."

"It's just . . ." I hesitate, trying to think up a good enough excuse. "A mess."

He walks ahead of me, ignoring my comment. "You should talk more, Fable. You've got a sexy voice."

I sigh heavily and follow him. My ground floor flat might not look like much on the outside, but inside, I've made it beat expectations. So, when I unlock the door and catch the surprise on Grizz's face, I smile to myself but block the way so he can't get past me. Once he sees the babysitter, he'll ask questions, and that's the last thing I need. "I have to see the rest," he tells me, trying to take a step forward. I block his move again, and he frowns. "I'll leave right after, I swear."

The living room door opens and I inhale sharply as Jessica enters the hall with Ivy in her arms. "I tried to get her to sleep, Luna, but she's stubborn," she teases. When she sees my horrified expression, she hesitates. "Sorry, am I interrupting?" Before I can reply, she backs into the living room and closes the door.

I wince before deciding the best course of action is to ignore what just happened. I kick off my shoes and shrug from my jacket, avoiding his eyes.

"Who was that?" asks Grizz. The words clog my throat, so I say nothing, hoping he'll just leave. "Is that kid yours?" He shakes his head, complete confusion across his face. "Nah, you can't have a kid. It's tiny." When I still don't reply, he pushes past me and heads into the living room. I groan and follow.

Jessica looks up in alarm, almost wilting when she sees the large biker filling the doorway. "Whose kid is that?" he barks. Her eyes glance my way, and he shakes his head again, moving so I'm blocked from her line of sight. "Nah, don't look at her for answers. Is it her kid?" I don't see Jessica's response, but I can tell by the way Grizz freezes that she's told him the truth.

"What does she owe you?" he snaps, pulling out his wallet. I try and move past him, but he doesn't allow it. Instead, he stuffs some cash into Jessica's hand and tells her to get lost. I give her an apologetic smile as she passes, placing Ivy in my arms. She'll probably never come back again after this.

"Does the Pres know about this, Fable?" he demands, watching me as I lower my daughter carefully into the Moses basket. I shake my head.

"Luna," I say quietly. "My name is Luna."

CHAPTER 2

GRIZZ

Luna. I like the way it rolls off her tongue. It suits her mystical vibe, and I don't know why she ever bothered to call herself Fable.

"Luna," I repeat, smirking a little.

She gives a small shrug of her shoulder. "My mum was a hippie."

"So, is the kid's dad around?" She shakes her head. "Why doesn't that surprise me? Is this why you've been avoiding the clubhouse?"

"It's not exactly good for my business," she mutters.

"The club's there to help," I tell her, knowing full well it's shit talk. None of the brothers are interested in the club whores' lives, but they sure as shit wouldn't touch her knowing she got caught out with a kid. Who knows if she did this shit to entrap some guy?

A realisation hits me. Lexi is right—we don't give a crap

about them, but they're real people with lives, just like us. I sigh. "Axel and Lexi have paired the brothers up with the . . ." I pause, not wanting to offend her.

"Whores," she says quietly.

I give a slight nod. "And luckily, you got me."

"Why is that lucky?"

"Come on, Fable, I know the other women talk about me. I'm never short of offers," I say, smirking. "I'm here to help out and get to know you," I peer into the Moses basket, "and this little one, I guess."

"Well, we don't need you," she replies, her tone almost a whisper.

"It's not a choice," I tell her firmly. "It's happening."

She fixes me with an annoyed glare. Fable's always been cute and smiley, but I guess that was all roleplay for the guys. "Fine," she says, heading for the door. I frown, glancing back at the baby. "You can watch Ivy while I sleep." And then she disappears, leaving me alone with her kid.

I pull out my mobile and put a call into Axel. He answers on the second ring, sounding sleepy. "This better be good."

"Did you know Fable just had a kid?"

I hear some rustling and a heavy sigh. "Nope."

"That's why she hasn't been around the clubhouse."

He clears his throat. "Wait, start at the beginning."

"What are you doing asleep anyway?" I ask, checking my watch. "It's almost one in the morning and you don't usually leave the office before three."

"Yeah, well, some of us have old ladies to keep happy," he mutters. "How old's the kid?"

I peer at the tiny baby, who is now awake and fidgeting. "I dunno, a few weeks maybe. How can you tell?"

"By asking?" he suggests.

"I would, but she's gone to bed and left me with the kid."

A laugh escapes Axel. "Wait, you're babysitting?"

I frown. "Yeah, that's messed up, isn't it? I'm gonna go give her the kid back and get out of here." I disconnect and stuff my phone in my back pocket. Then I stare at the baby some more. It's cute in a scrunched-up kind of way. I go to pick it up and realise I've never actually held something so small before, so my hands hover over it, trying to work out the best way to grip without hurting it.

I gently slide one hand under its tiny backside, then use the other to support the upper back and head and scoop it towards me. "Jesus," I mutter, holding it to my chest. "What the fuck is going on?" It makes a small sound, and I move quickly in the direction Fable went.

There are two doors that lead off from the hall. The first is a nursery, and I take a minute to appreciate the effort that's gone on in here. There's a painted mural on one wall with lots of little woodland creatures. It's unfinished, and the paint pots are spread out on a sheet covering the floor.

I go to the next room and stop in the doorway when I see a fully clothed Fable curled into a tight ball, fast asleep. "Well," I whisper to the kid, "looks like she's really tired."

I shift the baby so I'm holding it against me in one hand while I use the other to drag a blanket over Fable before backing out and pulling her door to. I'll let her sleep for a little while.

I head back into the living room and settle onto the couch, grabbing the television remote. "I was meant to be balls deep in Siren," I tell the kid, who is now snuggled against me with its eyes closed, "and instead, I'm babysitting a kid I don't even know." I give my head a shake. "You've cockblocked me and you're not even mine."

I wake with a start when the small bundle emanates a screech loud enough to wake the dead. "Jesus," I hiss, lifting it from my chest and staring at its red, screwed-up face. "Why are you making that noise?"

"She wants fed." I jump at the sound of Fable's voice, still not used to it. "She did well to sleep so long." She appears at my side, then she scoops the screaming alien from me and sits on the chair. I stare in amazement as she lifts her top and the sound immediately stops.

"You're breastfeeding?" I don't know why that surprises me, but it does.

Her cheeks redden slightly. "Just for a little while longer. I'll have to stop soon."

"Why?" The sound of the baby suckling fills the room and Fable looks down to watch, smiling. It's a beautiful sight.

"Because men don't want me leaking milk all over them," she says with a small laugh.

I frown. "Isn't it best for the kid?"

"She has a name," she tells me, a small smile still tugging at her lips. "Ivy. And they say breast is best, but formula-fed kids do just as well."

"But what do you wanna do?"

She thinks it over. "I like this bonding time," she admits, stroking Ivy's wispy hair, "but I need the money."

"How old is she?"

"Two weeks."

My eyes widen. "Two weeks? Are you even supposed to be back at work?"

Her smile fades. "Like I said, I need the money. Thanks for watching her last night. I shouldn't have done that to you. I didn't actually plan on falling to sleep. I thought you'd march after me, but when you didn't, I couldn't resist a little lie-down."

I push to stand. "No problem. Look, why don't you come to the clubhouse? Lexi might be able to help, and I'm sure Duchess will."

She shakes her head. "I have my family around here. I'm fine."

"Here's my number," I say, picking up her mobile and inputting my number. I call my phone so I have hers too. "If you need anything, call me." As I'm typing in my name, a message pops up on the screen from someone called Nate and my thumb catches it by mistake, opening it.

> Nate: Freebie. I'm bringing Dan now. Full works, Lu. I owe him big.

I pass her the phone. "Sorry, you got a text," I tell her, watching as she reads it.

She does well to compose herself, forcing a smile and laying the mobile on the table beside her. "Thanks again," she says just as Ivy pops off her breast, giving me an eyeful. I immediately look away, and Fable gives an awkward laugh. "Sorry," she mutters. When I turn back to her, she's covered.

"Who is that?" I ask, pointing to her mobile, because the message isn't sitting right with me.

She waves her hand in the air like it's nothing. "Business."

"It looks as though you're paying off someone else's debt."

"No, nothing like that. You should go. I have to get back into mute mode," she says, laying Ivy in her basket.

"And what about her?" I ask, nodding at the sleepy baby.

Her eyes fall to her daughter, and for a second, she looks sad. She takes a deep breath. "She's fine. She'll sleep now for an hour or so."

"You're just gonna be fucking in the other room while your kid sleeps in here?" I ask, unable to disguise the disgust in my voice.

Fable's expression hardens and she presses her lips together in a tight line. "And let Axel know I'm good without the bodyguard, or spy, or whatever it is you're doing here. Goodbye, Grizz."

I leave the flat, slamming the door behind me. It's selfish, but a part of me wants the kid to wake up so she can't be used the way she's clearly about to be. I'm crossing the carpark towards my bike when three men come around the corner laughing and joking. They're high and drunk, it's obvious by the way they're stumbling about and shoving into one another. I throw my leg over the bike and put on my helmet, watching as they go inside Fable's flat.

I grip the bars tight until my hands ache and then I start the engine and ride away.

It's none of my business what goes on in Fable's life, and she clearly doesn't want to have me involved.

LUNA

I gently rock Ivy, who woke the second Grizz slammed the door. *Prick.* The sudden raucous sound of laughter has me groaning in frustration. I thought a few hours of uninterrupted sleep might help, but I feel groggier now than before. I hear the front door open and then my brother appears in the doorway.

"Nate," I mutter.

"Get that thing to sleep," he mutters, dropping onto the couch. His two friends stay in the doorway, leering at me. "Then go do your thing. You got them both, right?"

I inwardly groan, but turning them away and making Nate look bad will cause all kinds of stress I don't need. It's been this way for so long, I know the drill. Denying my brother isn't an option. Ever. So, I force a smile and lay Ivy in her basket before heading for the bedroom.

This is my job. I repeat it as a mantra.

Reaching into the bedside drawer, I pull out two condoms, and before I can speak, Danny is on me like a dog. I hate kissing. It's something that stuck ever since I watched *Pretty Woman* and realised Vivian had a point—kissing is too intimate, and it should be for the one I love. However, it's easier said than done with eager men, so I wince while Danny takes full advantage of my mouth. His friend comes up behind us, and I feel his hands groping my breasts as his tongue runs along the side of my neck.

I gently press my hands to Danny's shoulders, and he pulls back, panting with need. "Easy," I say. "Let's just calm down."

He grins, his eyes turning cruel. "Easy," he repeats as his hand wraps into my hair, pulling my head back. "I'll show you fucking easy."

His friend unfastens my bra. "No," I say, trying desperately to keep it on. "I'm still feeding," I snap, batting his hands away.

"Even better," he whispers in my ear while grabbing my wrists and pulling them behind my back.

―――

I don't know how long I lie on the bed after they've left, but it's only when I hear Ivy crying that I come back into my own body and push myself to stand on shaking legs. I take my dressing gown from the floor and pull it on, catching a glimpse of myself in the mirror and immediately looking away in disgust.

I swipe an angry tear away and go into the living room. Ivy is kicking her legs and screeching, so I instinctively pick her up and hold her to me. Her mouth roots around, trying to find a source of food, and I shudder. I don't know if I'll ever get the feel of those men from my body and I haven't showered, so I head to the kitchen and get out a bottle. She squawks louder, getting impatient as I scoop formula into the bottle and add boiling water.

"Shhh," I hush, gently rubbing her back while her mouth furiously roots around my shoulder. My breasts begin to leak milk and it forces more tears from my eyes. "Please," I whisper, "just give me a second."

Once I've given the formula a shake, I run the bottle under the cold tap, praying for it to cool quickly while sobbing harder at Ivy's screams.

It's almost midnight when there's a knock on the front door. I freeze, wondering if Nate's brought more friends around, which he does often when he can't pay for his weed. My mobile alerts me to a text message.

> Grizz: I'm outside, let me in.

I frown before going to the door and opening it enough for me to peek out. I stare at him, and he stares back at me. "Well," he says impatiently, "let me in."

"No."

"What do you mean, no? Let me in, Fable."

"Luna. My name is Luna."

He shrugs. "Okay, Luna, let me in. It's fucking cold."

"Why are you here?"

"I told you already, Pres's orders. I went to Zen and Thalia said you called in sick."

"And I told you I don't want a babysitter. Go and watch over someone else." I try to close the door in his face, but he gets his foot in and it bounces back. "Fuck, Grizz, go home."

He gets his shoulder in and then begins to push the door until I can't hold it any longer, so I give up and move, letting it slam back against the wall. He gives a satisfied smirk and steps inside, closing it behind him. "Are you sick?"

"No, but in case you hadn't noticed, I've just had a baby and I didn't feel like fucking tonight, so if that's why you're here, piss off."

He raises his eyebrows, and for a second, I wonder if he'll yell. The bikers can get pissed if you take the wrong tone with them. Instead, he eyes me with concern, and somehow, that feels worse, so I go into the living room to break the moment.

He follows, leaning his shoulder against the door frame. "I just thought I'd check on you, make sure you're okay."

"As you can see, I'm fine."

He takes a step inside the room. "I think I preferred it when you didn't speak," he says cautiously.

"And I preferred it when Axel wasn't so nosey. Why is he really sending you guys out to check up on us?"

"I told you, Lexi came up with it. They want us to be a happy family."

"I have a family. I don't need another."

Ivy begins to cry from the bedroom, and we both turn our heads in that direction. "Fuck," I mutter. I only put her down half an hour ago, but she's been unsettled all day.

"You want me to get her?" asks Grizz.

I scowl. "No, just leave."

I go to the kitchen to get another bottle ready. A minute passes before Grizz appears holding Ivy. He's gently stroking her tiny head, and I marvel at how much smaller she looks cradled in his large hands. I give my head a shake. "I told you to go."

I begin running the bottle under cold water. "You made

the switch," he comments, and it makes me want to cry again. I'm not ready for bottle feeding and neither is she.

"Yeah," I say, my voice almost a whisper. I turn my back fully in case my tears fall.

"Weird," he responds.

"Why?"

"Well, this morning, you said you loved breastfeeding, and now, you're bottle feeding."

I shut off the tap and spin to face him. "Why do you even care?" I snap, and Ivy jumps in his arms. "Just go home and do what you do best—fuck a whore."

He lets me take Ivy from him but watches me with cautious eyes, like he's suddenly her protector. "I'm good here," he says, following me back into the living room and taking a seat. I move farther along the couch and place the teat into Ivy's mouth. She moves her head from side to side before finally sucking. "Did you pay the debt?"

I glance at him and then realise he's talking about this morning's text message from Nate. "Yah know, if anyone's talking shit about the club, it'll be London," I tell him, because let's face it, that's why Axel's got his beloved bikers on whore watch—someone's talking.

"What makes you say that?"

I shrug. "She's in everyone's business."

"If you know something, you should just come out and say it."

"I'm not talking to anyone about the club. I have too much going on in my life, so tell Axel I'm clean. Check my phone if you don't believe me."

He grabs my phone, and I roll my eyes. "Nate texts you a lot," he comments, scrolling through my phone.

"He's my brother," I snap.

"Makes sense," he mutters. I hate how he does that

without elaborating, so I wait a beat before turning to look at him again.

"What does?"

"You're doing favours for your brother. Drugs or gambling?"

"None of your business." I watch as he stares at my phone while tapping something into his own phone. "What are you doing?"

"Taking Nate's number."

My heart speeds up and I try to reach for my mobile, but he moves it away. "Why?"

"In case I need to call him."

"Why would you need to call my brother?"

"To arrange to meet him."

"I don't understand," I mutter. Ivy spits the bottle out and immediately cries. I sigh heavily, placing it on the table and lifting her to my shoulder to wind her.

"Feed her," he says firmly.

"I am feeding her."

"Feed her properly." I frown. "Breastfeed her."

"No. Look, I don't know what your problem is—"

"Prove to me you haven't stopped feeding her because those fuckers hurt you this morning," he barks, and I freeze. "Feed her."

I swallow the huge lump forming in my throat. If I don't feed Ivy, Grizz is going to call Nate, and that won't end well. "Weed," I whisper, answering his earlier question and hoping to avoid this confrontation. "He gets into debt over weed."

"Feed her, Luna."

I bite my lower lip, fighting back my tears. "But I don't mind," I whisper, the words sounding foreign as they come out broken. "He's my brother."

"Feed. Her," he says more firmly, and I can tell by the tone that he's losing patience. Ivy cries harder, and I'm unable to stop the fresh tears falling down my own cheeks.

I lay her in my arm and use my free hand to lift my top. Sickness swirls in the pit of my stomach, and I shudder as her mouth immediately roots around for her source of comfort. When she latches onto my breast, I cry out. It comes without warning, and I instantly stick my finger into her mouth so she'll release my breast. I hand her to Grizz and rush off to the bathroom.

CHAPTER 3

GRIZZ

I stare at Ivy, who's now screaming at the top of her lungs. She wants her mother, that much is clear, but I take the bottle anyway and stick it in her mouth. She suckles without a fuss, maybe because I don't smell of milk, and I relax back, watching her sweet, innocent face drink it down like a pro.

Once she's done, she releases her suction and falls into a milk coma. I stand and gently place her into the basket before going in search of Luna.

I find her in the bathroom, and I can hear her sniffles through the locked door. I tap lightly. "Open up."

"Is she okay?" she murmurs through sobs.

"Open up."

After a few seconds, the lock clicks and I push the door open. Luna stands before me with a tear-stained face and a red nose. I don't think too much about it as I pull her into my arms and hold her against my chest. Her small shoulders shake as more sobs leave her, and I gently shush her and tell her everything will be okay.

Ten minutes must pass before she lifts her head to look at me. "Sorry, I don't know what came over me."

"I'm guessing you don't wanna come back to the clubhouse?" I ask, and she shakes her head. "Which is gonna cause me a headache," I tell her, using my thumbs to wipe her wet cheeks. "How can I babysit you when you're here?"

"I told you," she says, wiping her nose on the sleeve of her top, "I'm fine."

"You look it," I say, my voice dripping in sarcasm.

"It's the baby blues," she whispers, leaning over the sink and splashing her face in cold water. Her shirt rides up her thighs, and I spot fresh bruises. I reach out, carefully running my finger over the largest, and she looks down. "I hit it on the table."

I take her hand, making her stand fully. She grabs a towel to dry her face as I take the shirt in my hands and pull hard, ripping it open. She gasps as buttons fly all over the floor, and I tug the shirt down her arms until it joins the discarded buttons and she's naked.

Her body is littered in blue and green bruises. It's impossible to see where one ends and another starts as I rake my eyes over her. When they finally reach hers, I see the pain in them. "What the fuck did they do?" I grit out, blood beginning to whoosh in my ears.

"It's nothing," she cries, and I turn to leave. I feel her hands wrapping around my wrist, trying to stop me. "Please, just leave it."

"Did you want them to do this?" I growl, turning on her. She shrinks back against the wall but doesn't release her death grip on me. "Did they do this with your consent?" Her mouth opens and closes a few times before she shakes her head. "Then let me go," I bark, trying to shake her off.

"Please, Grizz, you'll make it worse."

"Worse?" I lead her back into the bathroom and force her in front of the mirror. "Worse than this?"

She cries harder, her entire body shaking. "It's my life," she sobs. "It's what I do."

"No," I yell, gripping her by the shoulders and turning her to face me. "No, you choose. You say who, and where, and how much. You don't deserve this," I say, pointing to the bite marks on her stomach. "You can't even feed your baby because of them."

I shrug out of my kutte and place it on the side. Taking off my chequered overshirt, I wrap it around her then pull my kutte back into place over my white T-shirt. "Your fucking brother is selling you to pay his drug habit and that's not okay." She pulls my shirt around her, looking vulnerable and lost, and something in my chest tightens. "I'm sorry," I mutter, taking her hand in mine. "I shouldn't have shouted at you."

"It's just hard, yah know," she whispers. "He's so angry all the time."

"Your brother?"

She nods. "I don't want to upset him when he's around Ivy. It's not usually a problem, it's my job, but since having Ivy, I feel . . . different."

"So, come to the clubhouse. He can't get to you there."

She thinks over my words. "I like my flat, and my mum lives just upstairs. She needs looking after."

"Bring her."

She shakes her head again. "I can't. She won't come. I'm fine here, honestly. And I'm painting Ivy's bedroom." She gives a small smile. "I want to give her a home."

I tuck Luna's hair behind her ear. "I saw the room, and you're doing a great job, but you can do all of that at the clubhouse."

"I'll speak to my brother, tell him I'm not doing it anymore. I won't let him in the flat."

I sigh heavily. I can't force her to leave here, but I also know she won't stand up to her brother. "Fine. Whatever you want."

I lead her into the bedroom and pull the sheets back. "Get in," I tell her, and she does, slipping beneath the sheets and snuggling into her pillows. "Sleep."

―――

I slept soundly with Ivy in my arms for the second night running, and although I'd never admit it out loud, that kid is like a magical sleep guru. I ain't ever slept so well, and when Luna woke us both at six this morning, even she was surprised at how well her baby girl slept. But it meant I had to go for my workout, get back, and shower, all by nine, when the Pres called church. I made it just in time.

"So," he begins, "how's it all going?"

"London is a bitch, that's all I gotta say on the matter," mutters Cash, and a few of the brothers laugh.

"Foxy is great," Smoke says with a wink and a smirk. "Well, she was when I left her in bed a minute ago."

"Jesus, Smoke, you're not meant to be making them your old lady," says Fletch. "You'll give the others ideas."

"Anything suspicious?" asks Axel. The others shake their heads, and he waits for me to do the same. "VP?" he pushes.

"She got hurt yesterday," I say, staring hard at the club's logo carved into the centre of the oak table. I ball my fists as the anger returns. "How far are we taking this protection shit?"

"Hurt how?" asks Axel.

"Hey, Pres says she's got a kid," Duke cuts in. "When the fuck did that happen?"

"Can I end her fucking brother or not?" I spit, glaring directly at Axel.

"Clear out," Axel orders the others, and they do it quickly. He turns to me and repeats, "Hurt how?"

"Two guys—her brother's dealers, I think—raped her."

"Shit, is she okay?"

I shake my head. "No, but she won't come to the clubhouse, and she begged me to leave it, so I don't know what the fuck to do."

"Brother, if she wants you to leave it, you have to follow her wishes."

"And let them get away with it?" I snap, hardly believing my ears.

He shrugs. "If it's what she wants."

"She was upset and scared. She doesn't know what she wants."

"Grizz, she ain't your old lady. If you're feeling some kinda way, then—".

"I'm not," I say, irritated by his assumption. "It's not like that. But she's in a mess and her brother's a prick. He's getting her to pay off his drug debt."

"That's their business. These women all have lives outside of this club and it's up to them how much they share with us. If she's asked you to stay out of it, then you stay out of it. You can't wade in there, cos she might give you up to the police and then you'll be right back inside."

He's right. I've only just come off licence after being released from a five-year stretch in Belmarsh for assault. "Then what do I do?"

"You check in on her daily and keep an eye on things . . . and Grizz, if her brother turns up, you walk away. Are we clear?" I stare at him blankly. "Are we clear, VP?" I give a nod. "Good. I don't need you back inside over some club whore drama."

"I should get to the bar," I mutter, pushing to stand. "I've got a delivery coming."

He also stands. "How's it coming along?"

"Good," I tell him, a smile pulling at my lips when I think of it. "I can't wait for you to see it."

———

Danii is signing for my delivery when I arrive. She smiles as I get off my bike and hands the delivery guy his clipboard. "Nice of you to join us," she says, glancing at her watch, "at ten a.m."

"I got caught up."

"In someone's sheets?" she teases.

I smirk, pulling out the keys and opening the shutters. "You asking me something there, darlin'?" It's the second time she's inadvertently asked if I have a woman. When I glance back at her, she's blushing. "Cos you just gotta ask me outright. I don't do this flirting shit."

"Flirting?" she repeats innocently. "I wasn't flirting."

I unlock the door and push it open. She steps inside and watches as I begin to carry the boxes in, dumping them on the bar. "This place is just . . . stunning."

"You were asking me a question," I remind her.

"Was I?" She slides onto a barstool, and I place another box on the bar and send a smirk her way. It always works, and she almost melts as she admits, "I was. "Are you single?"

I laugh. "Now, why do you wanna know that?"

She rolls her eyes. "Cut the crap. We've been doing the dance for weeks now and you know it. I'm getting to the point because you're clearly not going to."

"And what point's that?" I step closer, and she inhales sharply as our legs brush.

"Do you want to go out for a drink sometime?"

"Yes."

Relief passes over her face. "Great. When?"

"Now," I tell her, reaching for a bottle of whiskey and holding it up.

She laughs, throwing her head back slightly to expose her neck, and I resist the urge to kiss her delicate skin. "I have a business to run."

"I forgot about that," I murmur, closing the gap between us and running my nose along her temple, inhaling her fresh scent. "So, when?"

She visibly swallows. "Tonight?"

"Tonight," I confirm, taking a step back. She releases a long breath, and I wink, heading out to grab the next box.

LUNA

I park Ivy's pushchair in the hall of my mother's flat and close the front door. It's cold, but then again, it's always cold. She refuses to top up the meter so she can heat the place. "Mum?" I call out.

I make sure the blanket is covering Ivy before heading into the living room. It's the same layout as my flat, only she hasn't cleaned it in a long time. There are burn marks in the old carpet that has been down since I was little, and I dread to think when she last ran a vacuum over the thing.

I find her on the couch, sprawled out and naked. Her body is covered in bruises too—*much like mine*—but I choose to push that thought away as I grab a dirty blanket from the table and place it over her. "Mum," I say, gently giving her a nudge. "Mum, it's lunchtime, wake up."

I remember the times I'd come home from school at lunchtime because I didn't have money to buy dinners and she was too proud to sign up for the free school meals option because she didn't want the teachers to look down their noses at us. She'd often be passed out like this, and sometimes there'd be a man with her, sometimes more than one. I shudder at the memories.

"Huh?" she mumbles, stirring.

"It's me, Luna. Are you hungry? I made some soup," I tell her, going back into the hallway to retrieve the bag containing homemade potato soup and fresh bread.

"Fuck off, Luna," she slurs, kicking the blanket from her body.

"You have to eat something," I remind her. "You'll end up back in hospital with pneumonia." She's spent more and more time there lately, and I often wonder if she does it to get a break from Nate.

"Maybe next time I'll die," she spits, sitting up and grabbing her pack of cigarettes.

"You're supposed to be quitting," I mutter, opening the soup flask and pouring a small amount into the lid for her to taste. She swipes it from my grip, spilling it over my hand.

"Fuck," I snap, dropping the lid to the floor. "Jesus, Mum, what's wrong with you?"

I place the flask down and grab the dirty sheet to soak up the mess. "Did Nate find you?"

I glance up. "No, why's he looking for me?"

"He needs money."

"Well, I don't have any," I tell her.

She sneers. "Is business slow? I told you that would happen if you kept the brat. You ruined my body, I couldn't get the same clientele after you." I remember the day I told her about the baby. She was so angry, not because she was worried for me, but she knew I'd need time off and she'd have to cover my time with Nate's friends.

"Have the soup," I mutter, pouring another cup. "Please."

"How is the brat?" she mutters, taking a sip and closing her eyes in pleasure.

"She's in the hall. You wanna see?" I go and get Ivy without waiting for an answer. "She's feeding from the bottle," I tell her proudly, tilting Ivy so she can see her. I long for her to be a good grandmother, to cuddle Ivy and coo over her like normal grandparents.

"Make the most of your tits while they're that big. You'll lose them if you stop feeding and they'll turn to saggy air bags." I roll my eyes. "I know a guy who sells photos. Shall I send him round to take some? He pays good."

"No, Mum. I don't want pervy Nigel taking photos of my boobs."

She shrugs. "Suit yourself. It would pay enough to get Nate off your back."

"Maybe Nate should sell his own pictures," I snap.

"He's your brother, it's your job to look after him."

"It's your job to look after him," I say, "but then you never did do that very well."

"If you've come here to insult me, Luna, you can just leave. I had Nate here last night with all his friends. I didn't sleep at all, and now, you're here giving me grief. Just get out."

"Nate's friends?" I repeat, taking in her naked state. "Mum," I sigh, "did you pay off his debt?" Usually, Nate saves his friends for me and brings older clients for Mum.

"He's a good boy. Not like you, you ungrateful slag."

I give a disappointed nod. "I'll come back tomorrow," I mutter, heading out. There's no point talking to her when she's like this.

Jessica turns up just after six, and I show her the formula. I was pumping my own milk before, but now I can't even bring myself to do that, so I go through how to make up fresh bottles.

By the time I get to Zen, it's six-thirty-eight and Thalia gives me a death glare. "You've got a client waiting in your room," she snaps. "You know how I feel about lateness."

I roll my eyes as I rush past her. "I'll give him a good show, he'll be fine."

Jimmy is already naked and wanking himself hard. I force a smile as I shrug from my coat. I'd usually do my makeup here and change before bringing a client up, but I get straight to it, beginning to strip from my clothing.

Working at Zen is easy money most of the time. Our clients are regulars, and apart from the smelly few, I don't mind any of them. Jimmy lost his wife a year ago. He's only forty-five and not bad looking, and it's a similar story to most of the men who come here. I don't talk to a lot of them, using the same strategy I use on the bikers, but with Jimmy, it's different. The first time I blew him, he burst into tears and told me all about his wife. I felt bad, and we spent the entire hour just talking.

"You're bruised," he says as I strip down to my underwear.

"Some clients like it rough," I say, pulling my hair back and tying it in place. "How have you been?"

"Worked up," he mutters.

I drop to my knees. "Let me help out there." I open a condom and roll it down his shaft.

I suck him into my mouth, and he groans before asking, "Do you think she can see?" I cup his balls, hoping we can get this done quickly. I'm starving, and I have soup in my bag. "Ellie," he continues. "Do you think she can see what we're doing?"

I let him fall from my mouth and gently push him to lie back. "Let's not think about it," I say, climbing over him.

"But if she could, she'd probably be pissed," he says, watching between us as I sink onto him.

"It's been six months, Jimmy. I don't think she'd be mad."

"You didn't know her. She was a fiery woman and so jealous."

I place my hands on his chest and begin to move, fucking him fast. "Oh fuck," I pant, like I'm having the time of my life. "Oh yes."

"Maybe she's with her mother," he says, panic on his face.

"Jesus, Jimmy, what's wrong with you tonight?" I ask, grabbing his hands and placing them over my bra. "I'm pulling out my best moves here, and you're thinking about your dead wife and mother-in-law watching us."

"Sorry," he mutters.

I turn so my back is to him and try again. Maybe if he's not looking at my face, he'll feel better. I grip his knees and sink down onto his cock. "That's it," I pant, "fill me up."

He comes hard a second later, groaning as I slow my movements. *Thank the lord.*

―――

I'm halfway through my soup when my bell rings, indicating my next client is coming up. I groan, placing the lid on my cup and rushing to the bathroom to brush my teeth.

"Why are you at work?" I huff out loud at the sound of Grizz's voice. "I went to see you and your babysitter answered. She's got a boy round there."

"So?" I mutter, going back into the bedroom.

"She's supposed to be watching Ivy, not canoodling with boys."

I smirk. "Canoodling?"

"You shouldn't be here after what happened."

I push the memories of Danny and his friend from my mind and sit in front of the mirror. "I have a client due."

"I'll give you the money," he says, and I frown. "If it means you take a few nights off to rest, I'll give you money."

"I don't need charity," I say, applying a little foundation to my skin.

"Fable—"

"Luna," I correct. "I'm only Fable when we're fucking."

"Jesus," he mutters, giving me that disgusted look again. "Please, will you take the night off and rest?"

"No." He sighs heavily and glances at his watch. "If I'm keeping you, feel free to leave."

"It's . . ." He trails off. "What time are you finishing?"

"Late."

"Luna," he snaps.

"I don't know," I say, shrugging. "Thalia is pissed I came in late, so she'll probably stick fat Malcolm on my list and he takes ages to finish." I notice how he balls his hands into fists, but he chooses not to comment. "Go about your business. I don't need a sitter, remember?"

He grumbles to himself and storms out.

After another half-hour, and once I've finished my soup, I head downstairs. Thalia looks up from her magazine. "Don't I have clients?"

"Not anymore," she says, arching a brow and going back to reading about celebrities.

"What's that supposed to mean?"

"By order of Grizz," she says, shaking her head in irritation.

"Are you kidding me?"

"Nope. He left me strict instructions to send your clients to the other girls," she slams her magazine shut, "like they haven't been covering for you enough."

"What?" I screech. "I need the money."

"Oh, he took care of that," she says. "He covered what you would've made and then some. He must've left a grand in your pot."

I rush out to the reception area and grab my pot. We

charge set fees and the club takes twenty percent. Our money is put into our own pots along with any tips. I pull out the roll of notes. "Jesus," I mutter. "What the fuck is his problem?"

"Maybe he's got the hots for you," Thalia singsongs. "It's about time he settles down."

"No, it's not that," I say on a sigh, keeping the money and heading back upstairs. I'm not sure what his game is, but it's definitely not that.

CHAPTER 4

GRIZZ

"You sure this is okay?" I ask, unlocking The Bar and letting Danii go inside ahead of me.

"It's fine," she says. "Who wants a posh dinner in a restaurant when you can have a drink here?"

I groan. "I've fucked up, haven't I?"

She laughs as I take her coat and place it on a bar stool. "No, honestly, it's fine. We said a drink, right, and this is a drink."

I pull out a chair, and she lowers into it. "Red or white?" I ask, grabbing a bucket and filling it with ice.

"White," she replies, and I grab a bottle from the fridge to pour her a glass. I stick the bottle in the bucket and carry them over to her. Placing the glass down and the bucket in the stand beside her, I whip out my lighter and light the candle between us. She flutters her lashes. "Candles? How romantic," she teases.

I go back over to the bar and measure myself a glass of

whiskey. "So, confession time," I tell her, "I've never done this." I join her back at the table and lower into the seat opposite. "Dates aren't really my thing."

She gasps in mock horror. "You're kidding, I'd never have guessed." She leans her elbows on the table and stares me in the eyes. "So, why did you agree?"

"I don't know," I admit with a laugh. "Something about you."

She groans. "Oh god, that's so cliché."

"It is," I agree, "but hear me out." She gives a nod, still looking amused. "Life in the MC isn't like life out here."

"Out here?" she repeats, arching a brow. "You sound like you're at war."

I give a humourless laugh. "Sometimes, but that's not what I mean. There are women on tap. I can click my fingers and get a woman, and that's not me being big-headed, it's just the life."

"Are you trying to warn me you're a player?"

I shrug. "I'm saying I've never needed to look elsewhere. But then you kind of popped up and it's made me think."

"Of?"

I take a drink of my whiskey to avoid the conversation getting deep. "For that answer, you'll need to have a few more dates with me."

She smiles wider, showing her perfect white teeth and cute dimples. "If that's your way of asking me out again, we'll have to wait and see how this pans out."

We talk, and it's nice to have a normal conversation about life and plans without it involving the shit from the club. She clears the bottle of wine before calling it a night, and I offer to walk her home. She doesn't live far, so within five minutes, we're standing outside her townhouse like teenagers, unsure of what comes next.

She presses her lips into a fine line to stop a smirk as we

stand awkwardly. "So," I mutter, stuffing my hands in my pockets.

"So," she repeats. "I'd invite you in for coffee, but . . ."

I'm already shaking my head because I decided on the walk here that I wasn't gonna repeat the same shit I always do. This time, I'm playing it right. "As much as I want to," I tell her, looking her in the eye so she can see I'm genuine, "I want to see where this could go."

She chews on her lip and gives a nod. "Okay."

"So, I'm gonna ask you again, and this time, I want an answer. Can we do this again?"

Her smile shines through. "I'd like that."

I bring a hand to her jaw and lean down to place a gentle kiss on her cheek. "Great. I'll talk to you tomorrow to arrange it."

I watch her walk up the path and go inside the house before I leave with the biggest smile on my face.

I head straight over to Luna's place, enjoying the short walk to clear my head. I knock on the door. It's a minute before it swings open and I'm faced with the sulky teenage babysitter again. I frown. "She didn't come home?"

The babysitter checks her watch. "It's only eleven. She's never home before at least midnight."

I push inside, ignoring her protests. I'm relieved to see the boyfriend's gone and Ivy is sleeping in her basket. "Okay, you can go." I pull out a twenty and hand it to her. She scowls at it like it's poison, and I sigh, adding another twenty. She stuffs the notes in her pocket and grabs her coat.

"Tell Lu her brother stopped by."

"What's his name again?" I ask.

"Nate."

"Do you know him?"

She gives a nod, and I follow her to the door. "Everyone knows Nate."

"How come?"

She gives me a look like I'm stupid for not knowing this prick. "He's just a wrong un," she says, and I frown. "Yah know, always in trouble and up to no good."

"Drugs?" I guess.

"And the rest. He thinks everyone likes him when, actually, everyone thinks he's a proper weirdo. He only gets respect cos of who he works for."

"Who does he work for?"

She rolls her eyes. "Are you a copper?"

I pluck at my kutte. "Do I look like one?"

She gives me another wary look before saying, "The Kings."

My frown deepens as she leaves. The Kings MC have their own patch on the other side of Manchester. Why would they be on our side? We've never had any problems with the club. In fact, last year, their President, Reaper, tipped us off that one of his members had gone into business with one of our bookmakers and they were skimming money from us.

I decide I'll raise it with Axel tomorrow, but right now, I need to find Luna. I call her mobile and she doesn't answer, so I immediately redial. I do it several times, and each time, she ignores my call.

Ivy begins to stir, and I scoop her up. "Be kind to me, kid. I have no idea how to make a bottle."

I head into the kitchen and find the powdered formula. I don't wanna get it wrong, so I put a call into the only woman I know will answer. "What?" Lexi mumbles sleepily.

"Hey, Lex, I need your help."

"Who the fuck's calling you?" comes Axel's voice.

"A man," she mutters, and I hear rustling.

"Who the fuck is this?" he barks into the phone, and I grin, contemplating if I should fuck with him.

"Who's this?" I ask.

"Grizz, you better have a good reason for calling my old lady when she's in my bed."

"Does she know how to feed a baby?" He groans, and I hear him pass the phone back to Lexi. "Do you know how to make up a bottle of formula?"

"Why would I know that?" she asks.

"I dunno, cos your sister had a kid?"

"I didn't feed it. Are there instructions?"

I turn the tin over in my hand and smile. "Yeah, good thinking."

"Great, goodnight."

"No, don't go," I say, and I begin to read the instructions out loud so she can help me.

"How old is the kid?" she asks.

"A couple weeks."

"Okay, so a scoop per ounce, that's two scoops and two ounces of boiling water. Then run the bottle under the cold tap to cool it."

"How do I know when it's cool enough?"

"Erm, taste it? You have to use a clean bottle, like it needs to be sterilised or something."

I give a nod even though she can't see me and open the cupboards again. I spot a basket with the label 'sterilised bottles' and smile. "Perfect. Okay, you can go now."

I make the bottle, and while I'm cooling it under the tap, Ivy begins to wail like a tiny devil. I smile as she goes red in the face cos, damn, it's the cutest thing I've ever seen.

I'm just settling into the couch with Ivy sucking on the bottle like a goblin when the front door opens and Luna appears. She frowns. "What are you doing here?"

"Where the fuck have you been?" I growl, keeping my voice low so I don't disturb Ivy.

"Is Ivy okay?" she asks, rushing closer. She gently runs her hand over Ivy's head. "Where's Jess?"

"If you mean the irresponsible teenager who lets her boyfriend round and then leaves the baby with a biker she doesn't know, she went home."

"Jess is great with Ivy. Do you know how hard it is to get a babysitter who works this late? You better not have scared her off."

"You won't be needing her anymore," I say firmly. "You're not working at Zen again."

She scoffs. "What?"

"You heard. You need to be here to look after Ivy."

"In case you didn't notice, I don't have money rolling in like you, so I can't afford to just stop working. Jesus, get off my case, Grizz, you're not my dad."

Her words piss me off. "Contact her father and ask for money. He should be paying for his kid."

"That's not possible," she mumbles, shrugging out of her jacket.

The bruises on her arms are turning a sickly shade of green and I eye them with contempt. "How can you go to work and fuck strangers after what happened?" I regret the words the second they leave my mouth because the look of hurt that passes over Luna's face is soul-crushing.

"Get out," she says.

I don't apologise, it's not something I ever do, so I narrow my eyes. "I paid you a night's money, so you didn't need to work tonight, yet you chose to anyway. Do you like those fuckers pawing over you?"

Her chest heaves as she tries to stay calm. "I want you out, Grizz. And don't come back."

Ivy releases her suction on the bottle, and I push to stand before placing her in her basket and covering her with the soft blanket. "By the way, your brother came to see you tonight. Jess was here alone." Something changes in her face and there's a flicker of panic in her eyes. "Is he dangerous, Luna?"

"If you don't leave, I'll call the police."

"I'm trying to look out for you," I hiss.

She puts her hand into her bag and pulls out the rolled-up notes I left in her tip jar. "Take this with you."

She shoves it hard into my chest, and as I take it, I grab her wrist and tug her closer. Her hands press against me and she stares up at me with a lost look in her eyes. My cock stirs, an instant reaction. "Axel told me to watch over you, and I always follow what my President says."

"Then I'll call Axel and tell him you're not wanted or needed," she snaps. "In fact, I'll cut ties with the club, and that way, Axel can stop worrying about me."

"You're so fucking annoying, do you know that?"

LUNA

There're sparks flying between us. It's not something I'm used to feeling, as getting paid for sex kind of turns the entire act into nothing more than a transaction. But with Grizz, there's tension and definite electricity. We're practically chest to chest —or head to chest in our case—and there's a definite bulge in his trousers, so I do something I've never had the urge to do before and throw myself at him. He catches me, and before he can question it, I kiss him. The last boy I wanted to kiss was when I was eleven years old, and that was a complete disaster because Nate found us and kicked off. Not long after that, I started working to bring money in. He said if I was old enough to throw myself at boys, I was ready for the real world. I never tried to kiss anyone again.

Our tongues tangle in an urgent dance of need. Grizz's hands cup my backside, and he walks with me until I'm pressed against the wall. He trails his kisses along my cheek, down my neck, and across my chest while he unfastens his jeans. He retrieves a condom from his back pocket, and I snatch it from him, sliding down his body until my feet are back on the ground. Taking him by the hand, I pull him to the bedroom. We're not even fully through the door before I'm ripping the packet and dropping to my knees. Grizz watches as I tug his trousers farther down until his erection pops free. I smirk up at him, remembering the last time we fucked was when he first got out of prison. It was hot, and I'd put it down to him not having it for five years.

I roll the condom over his cock and lick my tongue over the tip. He shakes his head, placing his hands under my arms to pull me back to my feet. "I need to be inside you, Fable," he murmurs. I don't take too much notice of the way he uses my club name. It's hard to get used to the change.

He walks me backwards until I fall back onto the bed and then he crawls over me like a prowling lion. I appreciate the way he avoids my breasts as he slides my top up my stomach and places kisses there. I reach between us to push my leggings down, taking my knickers with them. A second later, he's pushing into me and groaning in pleasure. His arms rest either side of my head, supporting his weight as he slowly withdraws and slides back into me. His pace is careful and gentle. He takes his time, occasionally dropping a kiss to my head or neck as he fucks me slow.

When he nuzzles into my neck, I turn my head slightly to capture his mouth with my own. The slow sex with kissing is everything I need right now, and I feel the build-up of an orgasm. It takes me by surprise because I don't come easily, and never during sex, except that one time with him. I fake it every single time with customers, and lately, the only orgasms I have are when I'm alone, and even that hasn't happened for some time because I'm too exhausted.

I grip his shoulders, scared to fully let go seeing as it's not happened before. He smirks, sliding a hand down to my thigh and hitching my leg up slightly so he's fucking me at an angle. He hits the spot immediately, and I arch my back while crying out in surprise. His mouth moves to my ear. "That's it, let go," he growls. "I need to feel you on my cock." His dirty mouth is the final straw, and I shake uncontrollably while the unfamiliar feeling rips through my body. He groans in satisfaction, briefly closing his eyes as my pussy clamps around him.

He waits for me to come back to Earth before pulling from me and tapping my arse so I turn over. I go onto all fours, but he pushes me flat and places his legs either side of mine. He's on all fours like a predator as he slides back into me. It must feel tighter this way for him because he moves faster, groaning and grunting with each thrust. Minutes later, he slams in hard and stills, shivering as he comes.

The only sound in the room is our pants as he flops down beside me. A second later, his light snores replace the heavy breaths, and I glance over to see his arm covering his eyes. I take in his jeans that are still halfway down his thighs and smile to myself. *Sex with someone I like is so much better.*

Grabbing the shirt he left me yesterday, I pull it on, then use a tissue to remove the condom and drop it in the waste bin. I slip from the bed and go to the bathroom to clean up.

I get Ivy's basket and bring it into the bedroom, then I slide back into bed and pull the covers over us both.

———

I wake with a start when Ivy lets out a scream. I sit up and look around the dark room, struggling to get my bearings for a second. Memories of Grizz fill my mind and I find myself smiling, until I feel the empty bed beside me and my heart sinks.

I turn the bedside light on and climb from the bed, picking Ivy up to comfort her. I check my phone for the time and see it's almost three in the morning. Ivy hasn't woken for a feeding during the night since Grizz began to sit with her. She must sense his loss like I do.

I head through to the kitchen to make her a bottle, pausing when I see the roll of cash I gave Grizz earlier. Next to it is a note. I snatch it up and glare at the words.

> Thanks. As we weren't at the club, I thought I should pay?

The words blur through my tears. Of course, he was using me. That's what I'm for, right? Club whores are for fucking, and as we weren't at the club, of course, he'd think about paying. After all, that's my line of work. I give my shoulders a shake and wipe my tears. *I don't know why I expected anything different.*

CHAPTER 5

GRIZZ

I felt bad leaving Luna in the middle of the night, but sleeping beside her didn't feel right and I couldn't move to the couch. I laid there for at least half an hour, hoping Ivy would wake so I could take her into the living room and sleep there. Then my mind got working and overthinking, so I decided to just get up and leave to avoid any awkwardness between us. Not that I think for one minute Luna would have felt awkward. It's not like we haven't fucked before—the only difference is I know more about her now and a small part of me felt like there was a connection. I laugh to myself, shaking my head. *A fucking connection? Who am I trying to fool?*

I increase the speed on the running machine and turn my thoughts off, concentrating on the pounding of my feet and the music blasting in my ears.

I get back to the clubhouse two hours later, shower and change, and go into Axel's office. "Pres," I greet.

He narrows his eyes. "You feed the kid in the end?" His tone is annoyed, and I smirk.

"I only know of Lexi," I argue. "None of the other women in my phone would answer if I called."

He grins at that. "I assume it was Fable's kid?"

I give a nod. "Never thought I'd say this, but she's fucking cute, man."

He arches a brow. "Don't be going soft on me, VP."

"It's her brother I came to talk about," I say, taking a seat. "His name is Nate and, apparently, he's well known on that estate. He works for the Kings."

This gets Axel's full attention. "What?"

"Weird, right? Why are they hiring from this end of the city?"

"You think they're making some comeback?"

I shrug. "I don't know, but I think we need to find out."

He gives a nod. "Keep a close eye on Fable and do some more digging."

I think about my next words carefully. "You reckon you could get Thalia to sack her from Zen?"

He fixes me with a stare before narrowing his eyes in suspicion. "Why?"

"She's been through some shit, and I don't think she should be working when she's got a kid at home."

"That's not your call, brother."

"You told me to look out for her, and that's what I'm trying to do."

"I told you to keep an eye on her activities. I wanna know if she's talking to people about the club. I don't care what she does for work or if she's got a kid."

"What would Lexi say to that?" I challenge. "Didn't she suggest this so we can be one big, happy family?"

"Are you trying to threaten me?" he asks, almost laughing.

I hold my hands up. "Of course not, Pres. Maybe I'll take this to Lexi, though, see what she thinks."

He scoffs. "I'll speak to Thalia. Maybe we can offer a very short maternity leave."

I smile as I stand. "Great, thanks, Pres." I head for the door. "I wanna do the opening for The Bar next weekend. What do you think?"

"I'll be there."

By the time I get to The Bar, it's mid-morning. I head right into the coffee shop, where Danii is chatting with a customer while she makes his coffee. I stand behind him, patiently waiting for my turn, and her eyes light up when she spots me.

"I was wondering if you're free for a drink sometime?" the guy asks.

Danii glances my way again, biting on that lower lip. I arch a brow, daring her to accept his offer, and her cheeks redden. "Actually, I'm not looking for anything right now, but thanks."

"Damn," he mutters, taking his coffee and tapping his card to pay. "When you change your mind, call me." He drops his business card on the counter and leaves.

I snatch it up before she can and screw it up, shoving it in my pocket. "Morning," I greet, winking.

"I believe that card was for me," she says, grabbing a takeout cup.

"You don't need it. Close up for an hour, let's eat lunch."

She looks around the empty shop then nods. I grin, going back to the door, turning the sign to 'Closed', and clicking the lock.

I take a seat, and she joins me with two slices of cake and

two coffees. "I'll pay so this counts as a date," I tease, and she smiles. *I love her smile.*

"Actually, I was wondering if you're free tonight?"

"Keen," I joke.

"I have this thing. It's not important, so if you're busy, I get it, but I . . ." She's waffling, and I laugh. "Sorry, I'm nervous."

"I'll be there."

"Oh, you really don't have to if you have plans. My family is crazy, and I just hate the thought of having to put up with them alone."

"Wow," I say, taking a sip of coffee. "Third date and I'm meeting your family."

She blushes. "You're right, it's a stupid idea."

I grab her hand and hold onto it. "I'll be there."

She beams and her blue eyes almost sparkle. "Thank you."

———

I feel weird without my kutte. I hardly ever leave the clubhouse without it, but tonight, I've replaced it with a half-zip jumper, and I didn't miss the way the guys all turned to look at me as I left. They wouldn't dare to comment, but I knew they were all wondering what the fuck was wrong with me. I look like a college prick going for an interview.

Lexi is at the gate speaking to Smoke, and I slow my bike until I'm beside her. "Fuck off," I tell the prospect, and he rushes away.

Lexi glares at me. "That was rude."

"I'm meeting a woman," I begin, and her eyes widen. "And her family." Her brows almost reach her hairline. "What do I talk about?"

"Erm, what do you know about them?"

"Nothing."

"Ask questions."

I give a nod. "Okay."

"But not like you're interrogating them. Maybe things like what they do for a living and ask if they enjoy it."

"Why?"

She stares at me for a second, and when she realises I'm asking a serious question, her frown returns. "Because it's polite to show an interest."

"Even though I'm not interested?"

She smirks. "Yes. Pretend you are." She straitens the collar on my plain leather jacket and brushes her hand over my half-zip. "You look smart. I like it."

"Is it too much?"

"No, it's perfect."

"Get over here so I can cut your hand off," Axel barks from the doorway of the clubhouse.

I grin, and Lexi rolls her eyes. "Don't curse," she whispers, "and always take the offer of a drink. It's seen as impolite to refuse."

I give a nod. "Thanks, Lex."

"No problem. And relax, they'll love you."

"One last thing," I say, pushing my helmet into place. "Don't tell anyone, including the Pres."

She salutes and heads towards Axel.

The traffic was mild compared to usual, and I arrive at Danii's within five minutes. I retie my hair because my helmet always messes it, and then I take a deep breath and head up the garden path. She opens the door before I knock, greeting me with a kiss to the cheek. She slips her hand in mine and it warms my heart as I follow her inside.

LUNA

I stare at Thalia, and she stares back. I guess it means nothing to her as I'll be replaced by the morning, but to me, it's my only escape. "I don't want time off," I almost whisper.

"It's not my call," she admits. "You're one of my best girls, so I'm as pissed as you, but Axel gives the orders."

"Bullshit," I snap. "You run this place and you banned him from overruling you."

"Well, some things he's very forceful on and this was one of them. Look, if you've got a problem, speak to him."

I grab my jacket. "Don't worry, I will."

By the time I get to the clubhouse, I'm wet through thanks to the downpour that began the second I left Zen. Smoke smirks as I stomp through the gate. "Not seen you for a while, Fable."

"Is Axel around?" I ask.

"In his office," he calls to me as I pull open the clubhouse door.

Cali gives a wave, and London saunters over. "Long time no see."

"I've been at Zen," I mutter. London's parents are loaded, so she doesn't have to work if she doesn't want to, which is why she can afford to hang around the clubhouse all day.

"Your bed's not been slept in for months."

"I had a kid," I mutter, passing her to go to the office.

"What?" she gasps. There's no point in keeping it a secret now. I'm sure Grizz has told the guys.

I knock on the door and wait for Axel to shout for me to enter. When he does and I go inside, Lexi is on his lap. She jumps up and rushes to hug me. "Where have you been?"

"Axel," I say, ignoring her as I disentangle myself from her arms, "I need my job back."

He smiles. "Fuck me, she talks."

"I'm serious," I snap.

He groans. "Not my call."

"Funny, that's what Thalia said, and she told me to speak to you."

"What's happened?" asks Lexi.

"Club business," snaps Axel, and she turns to him with a raised brow.

"Thalia just sacked me from Zen."

"Not sacked," Axel corrects. "You're getting basic pay."

"I can't live on basic pay, Pres. I need the tips."

"I'm just following my VP's wishes."

"I should've known," I mutter.

"Grizz asked you to sack Fable?" Lexi asks.

"Not sacked," Axel repeats, sounding irritated. "She's on maternity leave."

"Fine, where is he?"

"Ask my old lady. I've been asking the same since he hightailed out of here earlier following their secret chat."

"Grow up," snaps Lexi. "It wasn't a secret chat. He asked for advice."

"First, he calls you in the middle of the night, and now, he stops to talk to you at the gate. I wanna know where my VP is."

"So do I," I snap.

She groans. "Fine. He's on a date." I inhale sharply, ignoring the twist in my heart. "But you can't say anything cos he doesn't want anyone to know."

Axel laughs hard. "Fuck off. Grizz doesn't date."

"It's a bit beyond that, I think," she says with a grin. "He's meeting her family."

"I'll go," I mumble. "I'll call him later."

"Wait," says Lexi, hooking her arm in mine. "Stay for a drink or two and say hello to the girls. We've all missed you."

One drink turns to two, then three, and by six, I'm not thinking about Grizz anymore. It's been good to laugh with the girls again. I've missed this.

I'm at the bar when Fletch comes up behind me. He's fairly new to the club, having transferred from another charter. His hands take my hips and he rubs himself against me. I roll my eyes, even though he can't see my face. "I need company," he growls in my ear.

I try to dodge his mouth, and he runs kisses down my neck instead. I shake my head and offer a sweet smile instead. "Aww, come on, Fable. I need the peace you bring me."

Placing a hand on his cheek, I give him a quick kiss on the other cheek and step around him, but he grabs my wrist and tugs me into his arms. "You know how sexy it is when you're all mysterious like this?" He wraps his large arms around me again and presses his erection against my stomach.

His hands wander up my shirt until he's cupping my breasts while nipping at my neck. I close my eyes and think about Grizz's hands on me.

Fletch lifts me onto the barstool and stands between my legs, retrieving a condom from his back pocket. It's not unusual for the men to fuck in the main room. It wasn't too long ago we were required to walk around here naked or just in underwear.

He makes quick work of releasing his erection and fisting it a few times before ripping the condom open. "I'll be quick," he mutters, sheathing his cock. His mouth goes back to my neck, and I hold onto his shoulders while he pushes my skirt up higher and moves my knickers to one side.

"What the fuck is going on?" growls Grizz, appearing in my eyeline behind Fletch.

The hurt knowing he ran out on me last night, and knowing he's been on a date, hits my chest again. I pull Fletch's attention back to me, cupping his cheeks with my hands and kissing him. It feels wrong. Most of the guys know I don't kiss, so his surprise shows in the way he stiffens against me, but it only takes him seconds to get lost in it. I keep my eyes fixed to Grizz as he folds his arms over his chest and arches a brow.

"I asked a fucking question," he barks, and Fletch pulls back.

"Sorry, VP," he pants. "Is this urgent? I'm in the middle of something here." I pull him closer, and his erection pushes at my entrance. He closes his eyes like he's in pain, and I smirk. "Seriously, bossman . . . please, can it wait?" he almost begs.

"No, it fucking can't. Put your dick away now." Fletch groans but does as asked. I jump off the stool and pull my skirt into place.

Before I get chance to walk away, Grizz takes me by the upper arm and guides me outside. "Would it kill you to keep your fucking legs closed?" he spits, shoving me to walk in front of him. Whenever I try to go back into the clubhouse, he shoves me again until I finally give up and head for the gates. "Home. Now."

"Fuck you," I spit.

"We did that part."

I cross my arms over my chest and march in the direction of home with him tailing me, silent all the way.

He follows me into my flat despite my protests and throws some cash at Jess. She leaves, and he goes into the bedroom to check on Ivy. I go to the kitchen and grab a glass of water. He still looks pissed when he joins me, which only makes me angrier. He has no right to be angry.

"Thalia sacked me today, but you already knew that."

"You're on maternity leave like other working mothers," he snaps.

"I can't afford to live," I yell, taking him by surprise. "Stop interfering in my life."

"Stop fucking it up," he yells back, only louder. "You're a mother now, act like it."

"I'm a good mum," I argue.

"Of course, you are," he sneers. "Mother fucking Teresa."

"You didn't seem to mind last night," I hiss, grabbing my money jar from the cupboard and taking out the roll of cash. I throw it at him and it hits him in the eye. "Consider last night a freebie. I felt sorry for you."

He gives an unamused laugh. "I don't need a pity fuck from a club whore."

"You seemed pretty desperate last night."

"I must've been to put my cock anywhere near you after the amount of pricks you get a day." I roll my eyes. He's just like the rest—a typical man who insults my job the second he gets a chance. I don't know why I thought he was different. "I think I preferred it when you didn't speak," he adds.

I give a slight nod. When I didn't speak, things were so much easier, so I push past him and go through to the bathroom. When I try to close the door, he sticks his foot there. "We haven't finished."

I have nothing left to say to him, so I begin to strip out of my wet clothes. He's seen me naked a million times or more, so I'm not embarrassed as I turn on the shower and step into the steam. I scrub my body until it's red, the same way I do every night. When I step out, he's leaning in the doorway, watching as I dry off.

"I don't like it when we fight," he mutters. I take my body butter from the cupboard and open it. "And I like hearing your voice." I scoop some of the strawberry butter and lift my leg onto the closed toilet seat, rubbing circular motions along my thigh and down my leg. "Luna," he whispers, "please."

When I continue to ignore him, he steps closer, taking the pot of cream from me and scooping a handful. "I just want to take care of you." He rubs the cream between his palms and then runs his hands down my arms. He takes each at a time and massages the cream into my skin. I watch him scoop some more, warming it in his palms before rubbing it over my chest and into my breasts. I close my eyes, loving the feel of him again. He moves down my stomach and crouches before me, scooping more cream and rubbing it into my other leg. When he stands, his erection is pushing against the denim of his jeans. He turns me away, and I stare into the mirror, mesmerised by the way his hands run over my shoulders and down my back. He pays extra attention to my backside, and when he moves closer, pressing himself against me and burying his nose into the crook of my neck, all my anger disappears. He bends me over the sink and runs his hand through my wetness. "Are you wet for me . . . or Fletch?"

"You," I whisper, closing my eyes when he pushes a finger into me. I grip the sink and rest my head on my arm.

I hear the condom wrapper and then he's back behind me, pushing his erection against my opening. He lifts one leg, holding it against his thigh as he slips into me, pushing deeper than he'd gone before until my knuckles turn white from my death grip on the sink. "Take it all," he murmurs, inching in farther. "Fuck yeah."

His hand finds my breast and he cups me, ignoring the milk leaking. I try to push him away, but he drops my leg and uses that hand to hold my arm up my back. "It's natural," he pants. "And I like it," he adds, using the wetness to tease my nipple. "Don't push me away again."

I'm close to an orgasm, so it pisses me off when he pulls out and sits on the toilet seat. He guides me to straddle him and holds my arms behind my back. "Fuck me," he orders. I begin to move, and his mouth goes to my nipple. He licks the swollen bud, keeping his eyes on my face to see my reaction. When I groan in pleasure, he does it again. It spurs me on, and I move faster, chasing the release I desperately need. His hands release my wrists and go to my throat. He applies pressure, staring down at our connection and groaning as I ride him. I jerk as the first sign of an orgasm hits me, and he stands, keeping our connection.

"You can't come yet, I need more," he growls, carrying me to the living room. He lays me on the couch and pulls from me, crouching down between my legs to swipe his tongue through my wet folds. I buck against his mouth, and he cups my backside, forcing me to keep still as he eats my pussy. I quickly come apart, shuddering uncontrollably.

Grizz crawls between my legs, wiping his mouth on the back of his hand before sinking into me. He turns us so I'm on top, riding him. I watch as he comes apart, growling from somewhere in the back of his throat and clenching his jaw. It's fucking hot, and when he's done, he pulls me down to kiss him. It's slow and sexy as our tongues twist together.

I lie against his chest, and he wraps his arms around me. My eyes suddenly feel heavy, and although I don't want to fall asleep with him still inside me, especially after our argument, I find myself drifting off.

When I next wake, I'm in bed with Grizz lying behind me. His cock is nudging at my entrance again, and I don't bother to resist as he pushes into me. He positions me on my stomach, placing one hand over my mouth to keep me quiet, the other gripping my hip as he slams into me. It's hot and fast, and when he's finished, he wraps me in his arms, and we fall back to sleep feeling satisfied.

CHAPTER 6

GRIZZ

I work out extra hard in the gym, with thoughts of Luna and Danii on my mind. I snuck out of Luna's at five a.m., after giving Ivy a bottle and putting her back to bed. Luna didn't stir once, but then, I did wake her twice during the night. I smirk at the thought. I left her a note to tell her I'd fed Ivy at five and I'd be back later to see them both. If she knows I'm coming back, maybe she won't try to get her job back from Thalia.

I'm in the steam room when Axel turns up. He grins, and we fist-bump. "Before you give me shit, I haven't come for a workout," he says, sitting down and resting his head back.

"You're late anyway. I did two hours before coming in here."

He rolls his eyes. "You work out too hard."

"You don't work out enough."

"I got some information out of Lexi last night," he says with another smirk.

I groan. "I knew she couldn't keep her mouth shut."

"She had no choice. I basically accused you two of having an affair."

I glare at him, and he laughs. "Brother, I know you wouldn't go there, but it got me the information I needed, and then she spent the night giving me makeup sex to prove she's only got eyes for me."

"You're a narcissistic prick," I tell him.

"How did it go, and why the hell didn't you want me to know?"

"Cos I wanted to avoid this bullshit," I say.

"Who is she?"

"No one you know."

"Brother," he says, sounding exasperated, "come on, give me something."

"She works near The Bar," I mutter reluctantly. "We've had a few dates."

"Fuck," he says with a shit-eating grin. "You like her."

"Don't be a dick."

"You do, cos you're keeping her from the club. You don't wanna scare her off."

"Well, she's gonna be at the opening, so there'll be no more hiding her."

"That's great, brother. I'm pleased for yah. What's her family like?"

I smile at the memory of last night. "Nice. Welcoming. She's got her parents and two sisters. They look like a normal family."

"Good. Did Fable give you shit last night?"

My smile falters. "I caught her almost fucking Fletch on the bar."

He stares at me for a long minute. "What's going on there, brother?"

"Nothing," I say a little too quickly, "but she should be resting after having the kid. The brothers need to lay off her."

"She's free to say no at any time," he says. "Was Fletch outta line?"

I shake my head. "No, nothing like that."

"I'll speak to the guys, make sure they check she's okay before they do shit."

I give a nod, hating the thought of my brothers being with her. "And for the record, she likes being called Luna."

"Why?"

"That's her name, dickhead," I say with a grin. "I like it."

"I reckon you like way more than her name," he says, his tone teasing.

I give my head a shake. "Nah, it's not like that, Pres. She's a mess, barely looking after the kid, and she's got no money. I don't need a reminder of my own mother."

"Which is why you're dating a mystery woman with a good family?"

I give a nod. "Exactly. She's a businesswoman and has her head screwed on right. She'll be good for me. I'm just helping Luna get back on her feet so she don't let that baby down."

———

This time when I walk into her shop, Danii has my coffee waiting. I smile, grabbing it from the counter and taking a seat while she finishes up dealing with the line of customers.

When she joins me, she kisses me on the cheek before taking a seat. "What was that for?" I ask, smiling.

"My family loved you. I wanted to say thank you for coming, I know it was a weird request, but it gets them off my back for a while."

"They seemed nice," I comment, sipping my coffee.

"They were quizzing me after you left. My parents were so

impressed when I showed them pictures of the work you did in The Bar."

"You took pictures of my work?" I ask, laughing.

"I don't know if you're aware, but you're amazing with your hands." She blushes when she realises her words, and I smirk. "Oh god, I'm so embarrassing."

I laugh harder, taking her hand and tugging her closer. "You're perfect," I say, kissing her on the nose. She stays close, bringing her eyes to mine. She wants me to kiss her, it's written all over her flushed face, and I almost do. My lips are a breath from hers, but Luna appears in my head. I pull back and take another sip of coffee. "Have you been busy today?" I ask, looking around.

She looks disappointed as she sits back in her seat. "Erm, yeah, rushed off my feet."

"That's good."

"Yeah."

We fall silent, and I inwardly scold myself for being a pussy. There's no future for me and Luna. But Danii, she's different. I *should* be kissing her. We've been on three dates, and I've met her goddamn family, so what the fuck is stopping me?

I stand abruptly, taking her by surprise. "I better get on."

She gives a nod. "Okay. See you soon?" She sounds hopeful.

"Yeah, sure."

She frowns. "Sorry, but what happened?"

"Huh?"

"Just there," she mutters. "You just withdrew right in front of my eyes, and I don't want to be that girl but . . ."

I panic. She's calling me out on my shit, and instead of being honest, I lean in, pinching her chin between my fingers to tilt her head back, and I kiss her. It steals her breath, and her hands go to my shoulders. The kiss is slow and sexy, and I have to picture Axel to stop my cock embarrassing me. I pull back, and she smiles, her cheeks flushed. Oh," she whispers.

"I can't take you out tonight, but the opening is this weekend. Will you come?"

She nods, smiling wide. "Yes, I'd love to."

I place a gentle kiss on her lips. "Good. Eight o'clock."

I find Luna in the kitchen when I get to her place later that day. I follow the sound of her singing, noting how beautiful her voice is. Leaning in the doorway, I watch as she presses something gooey on the worktop while singing a nursey rhyme to Ivy, who's also on the worktop in a bouncy seat.

I clap my hands, and she jumps in fright, laughing with embarrassment when she realises I heard her singing. "You shouldn't sneak in like that."

"You should keep the door locked."

She glances at her watch. "You're early today. We don't usually see you until late into the evening."

I go over to Ivy and gently bounce her chair. "I finished at The Bar early, thought I'd stop by to make sure you don't try to go into work."

"I'm giving up on that," she tells me, working her hands into the puffy dough. "I figured you'd soon get bored of watching me, so until then, I'll just wait."

I smirk and nod at her hands. "What are you doing?"

"Bread," she says, frowning like I'm clueless. "Haven't you ever made bread?"

I scoff. "Do I look like I've made bread? In fact, you don't look like you make bread."

"I always make my own bread," she says, looking a little insulted. "You don't know anything about me, Grizz. I might actually surprise you." I rub my hands over my tired face.

That's what I'm afraid of. "As you can see, I'm safely here at home, where you want me to be, so you can go about your life."

I snigger. "That's exactly what you want, for me to think you're behaving so I'll leave you alone."

She puts the dough into a tin and shoves it in the oven. "Haven't you got plans tonight?"

I narrow my eyes, wondering if Lexi mentioned my date to Luna. It doesn't matter—Luna knows the score.

"Nope. I'm free as a bird."

"Well, I'm not, so go and make yourself busy." I watch her take a different tin from the oven as the smell of freshly baked bread hits me. My stomach growls loudly and she laughs. "Have you eaten?" I shake my head. "Sit down."

I slide into the seat as she cuts a chunk of bread from the loaf, then she adds butter and hands it to me. I inhale the yeasty, buttery goodness and take a large bite, closing my eyes as my taste buds light up. "Jesus," I mutter around a mouthful, "that's amazing."

"I like to experiment," she says, smiling shyly. "It's got a hint of red chilli." She slides a pot of butter my way. "And this is homemade garlic butter. Dip it," she urges, nodding at me excitedly. I dip the warm bread and take another bite. It's exceptional, and she smiles proudly at my groans of pleasure.

"You could sell this," I tell her, reaching across to grab the loaf so I can rip more from it. She glows under my praise and it tugs at my heart.

"Try the olive one," she says, sliding a cupboard open and taking out a fresh loaf.

"How much bread do you have hidden away?" I ask, grinning.

"I make it for the church," she says, cutting a slice and passing it over. She's right, it's even better. "And I take some to my mum."

"The church?"

"They feed families that can't afford to eat."

It drags memories from my own childhood and I give my head a shake to clear them. "Do they pay you?"

She laughs. "No. And I wouldn't take a penny if they offered. They're doing it out the goodness of their hearts. There are loads of volunteers who help out. It's where I'm heading now. Actually, would you watch Ivy for two minutes while I get changed?" I give a nod, and she rushes off.

I sigh heavily and gently stroke a finger over Ivy's cheek. "Now what, little goblin? Why's she gotta be baking bread and helping others like Mary damn Poppins?"

LUNA

I pull on a hoody and some jeans then stick my feet into my tatty trainers. Grizz looks me up and down, and I wonder what he's thinking. I'm not sure he's seen me in normal clothes. I take the fresh loaf from the oven and tip it into a box for my mum.

"Sorry I've got to shoot off," I tell him, taking Ivy from the chair and carrying her to her pushchair in the hallway, "but thanks for stopping by."

"I'll come," he blurts out and immediately frowns like he didn't mean to offer.

"It's fine. You must have things to do," I say, tucking Ivy under her blanket.

Grizz leans over. "Will she be warm enough in there?" he asks, checking the thickness of the blanket.

I laugh. "Yes. I have this too," I say, holding up the thicker blanket. He takes it from me and covers her over. I can't help the way my heart squeezes at how he fusses over her.

I grab the bread boxes and stick them under the pushchair,

and when I open the door, Grizz takes control of the pushchair and I follow him with a smile on my face.

We get in the lift, and he screws his nose up at the smell of urine. "You get used to it," I tell him, laughing.

"She shouldn't breathe it in," he mutters, nodding to Ivy.

We go up to the next floor and move along to Mum's flat. "Wait here," I tell him, pushing the door open.

He ignores me and follows me inside. I inwardly groan, praying she isn't in a mood today. I take a loaf and go into the living room, hoping she's asleep so I can just dump it and run. I freeze when I spot Nate and his friend on the couch smoking a joint. Mum is in her underwear, and for a second, she looks relieved to see me. "Here she is, Perfect Polly with her loaf of bread," sneers Nate.

I place it on the table. "Are you okay, Mum?" I ask.

I feel Grizz's presence behind me. It was too much to hope he'd stay in the hall. Nate's eyes look past me to the man-mountain now filling the doorway. "Yes, love, I'm fine," she answers, her eyes also fixed behind me.

"I topped up the gas key," I tell her, producing her key and sticking it in the gas meter, "so you can put the heat on."

"Aren't you going to introduce us?" asks Nate, glaring at me.

"Mum, eat something," I say as I stuff the gas key back in my pocket. There's no point in me leaving it here, she'll only lose it.

Nate stands, blocking my path, and I sense the way Grizz suddenly stiffens, his eyes fixed on my brother's back. I give my head a slight shake, wanting to avoid any trouble. "I'm Grizz," he announces, dragging Nate's attention back to him. He moves forwards, holding out his hand. Nate takes it, and they shake.

"What are you doing hanging round my sister?"

"Just passing through," says Grizz.

"You're a Chaos Demons biker," says Nate, glancing at the patch on Grizz's kutte. "Why are you sniffing around Lu?" Nate throws a protective arm around my shoulders, and I automatically flinch. Grizz doesn't miss it and his eyes narrow.

"Like I said, passing through."

"Her bedroom?" he pushes.

"Jesus, Nate, he's one of my bosses from Zen. Relax," I snap, shrugging him away. "He came to see me about some extra shifts and saw me struggling with the pushchair."

Nate gives a slight nod. "Don't do too many extras. When will you fit my lads in?"

I head for the door. "Okay," I mutter.

We get outside, and Grizz is staring at me as I press for the lift several times. "His lads?" he asks.

"It's a side hustle."

He pinches the bridge of his nose. "Of course."

We walk to the church in silence. I'm so lost in my thoughts, I don't have the words to make him see it's not my choice. But I can't have Nate bringing his friends around on a regular basis. Not with Ivy in the flat.

We enter the church and it's bustling with people. The vicar spots me and rushes over, embracing me and turning to Grizz to shake his hand. "This is my friend, Grizz," I explain as I offload bread into his arms.

"You're very lucky to have such a wonderful friend in Luna," the vicar tells him. "She's been sent from Heaven especially to help us."

I laugh, rolling my eyes. "He's being dramatic," I tell Grizz.

"She never lets us down. We rely on her breadmaking skills," he continues, and we follow him to the row of tables where large pots of food are presented. He places the breads and dips at the end, and people immediately line up to get some. "See," says the vicar, laughing, "I think half these people come especially for Luna's bread."

He wanders off to help serve, and I begin to stack dirty dishes into a bucket. "What about Ivy?" asks Grizz, glancing into her pushchair.

"She's fine. She'll sleep."

He follows me to the kitchen, carrying another two buckets of dishes. "So, you come here every day?" he asks, watching as I roll up my sleeves.

"Every Wednesday," I tell him, turning on the hot tap. "I wish we could do it every day, though, cos this area needs it. But everything is voluntary, even down to the food. We rely on people cooking and donating."

He stares out the hatch to the room of families all enjoying a hot meal. "I used to come to a place like this when I was a kid," he mutters. "Not with my family. On my own."

"They're essential," I say, not wanting to push him in case he doesn't want to give me details. "They've helped me so much."

He turns back to me. "How long has your mum been like that?"

I shrug, dunking some plates into the soapy water. "A long time. Worse since my dad left."

"Everyone thought you were from a good family."

I feel shame wash over me. "I lied. One of the guys asked me one night and it caught me off guard. I told him I'd lied to my family, who thought I was an accountant." I shrug. "It's stupid, I know, but I wanted to feel normal for once. Like I actually came from a really nice family."

"What happened to your dad?"

"He left. Ran off with Mum's friend. She was devastated, and she slipped further into depression. We never heard from him again, but he left us with a load of his debt."

"Debt?"

I begin to stack the clean dishes while he grabs a towel to dry them. "He was a gambler, drug user, alcoholic. When he left, his debts transferred to us."

"Did you pay them?"

I give a nod. "Kind of. Mum and I worked hard. Nate not so much. I think he made the debt worse."

"Do you know who the debt was owed to?"

I shake my head. "Mum never went into detail. I was only eleven or twelve when he left."

"How did you pay the debt?" he asks, frowning.

I scoff. "How I always pay debts, Grizz."

He freezes, his eyes burning into me. "You sold yourself at twelve?"

"Of course. How do you think I got into this mess?"

He shrugs. "I never really thought about it."

I laugh. "Do you think I turned eighteen and decided I wanted to prostitute myself as an ambition in life?"

"When you put it like that . . ." he mutters, looking troubled.

"My family was in a mess and I didn't know any better. I'd seen my mum do it a thousand times cos she wasn't shy about having sex. She'd have sex with my dad's friends or dealers so he could have a free fix."

"Jesus," he mutters, shaking his head.

"It happens more than you think," I tell him.

"Don't you want different for Ivy?" he asks, and I stop what I'm doing and stare at him.

"Of course. I'd never let anyone lay a finger on Ivy. I love her with all my heart and I'm doing everything I can to get myself out of that flat and to somewhere better."

"And safer," he cuts in.

"It must be easy for you," I mutter, going back to washing the plates. "I bet you don't go to bed hungry or lie awake worrying about how to pay the rent."

"Not anymore," he says, "but I did. When I was younger. You know, there's a place at the clubhouse."

I scoff. "You really believe that, don't you?" I snap. "You keep offering it like it's a lifeline."

"Isn't it?"

"No, Grizz. I'm no safer at the clubhouse. Yes, Nate's friends won't turn up and do shit I don't wanna do, and the brothers won't force themselves on me, but I still have to give myself over. And it's for free. I don't make any money yet I'm expected to perform whenever a man wants me to, sometimes more than once a night. I can't have Ivy lay in my room while men are visiting me."

"That's what's keeping you from coming to the clubhouse?"

"Not just that. I want independence. I don't want to rely on a man to keep me safe. I'm Ivy's mum, she should be able to depend on me."

"And she will. Come to the club, get yourself straight, and then find somewhere to live. I'll make sure none of the brothers touch you."

"How?" I demand. "You know the rules. Unless I'm an old lady, I'm fair game. You can't keep them away from me."

"I'll speak to Axel."

I give up because he's not listening to me. "What I need is a job."

He gives a nod. "We'll look at some later. I'll grab my laptop."

CHAPTER 7

GRIZZ

On our way back from the church, we stop by the club to grab my laptop and head back to Luna's. I also bring an overnight bag, figuring if I stay over, I can make sure her brother's friends stay away.

I offer to feed Ivy as she sets about tidying up her kitchen, and when she's done and Ivy is sleeping, I grab the laptop and we sit on the couch. "Okay," I say, "what sort of job?"

She shrugs. "Anything."

"What experience do you have?"

She frowns. "I'm only good at one thing."

I narrow my eyes. "Bullshit, Luna. You just made a shit load of bread."

"I'm not a qualified baker. I won't get a job in a real bakery or anything."

"So, tell me all the things you're good at."

She sighs heavily. "I make bread and I have sex. There is nothing else. Maybe I could stack shelves or something."

My heart sinks a little at how much she doubts herself. "Fine," I mutter, entering the job into the search engine.

She peers closer as a list of vacancies pops up. "Jesus, that's not much per hour."

"Minimum wage," I say with a shrug. "I could ask Axel if there's anything going in any of the businesses."

She shakes her head. "No, I'll find something."

"There's no shame in getting help once in a while, Luna."

"I know. I just can't see me finding anything with good hours that I can fit around Ivy. Jess can't babysit during the daytime, she's at school."

"Which proves she's not old enough to watch a newborn."

"Have you seen how much childcare is?" she asks, arching a brow. "I could never afford that, especially if I take a job paying minimum wage."

"I feel like you're trying to prove to me that working at Zen is the best for you."

She gives a small grin. "Is it working?"

I shake my head. "You need to tell Ivy's father and let him provide."

Luna looks pissed as she stands. "I'm not relying on a man."

"That's ridiculous," I tell her, grabbing her wrist before she can go anywhere. I place the laptop on the table and pull her onto my lap. "It's about getting money you're entitled to for Ivy."

"He'll want to be in her life. I don't want to share her."

"That's just selfish."

"I'm protecting her," she snaps, trying to get out of my hold. Her fidgeting only arouses me, and I pull her closer, burying my nose in the crook of her neck. "I won't have a man letting her down."

"He might surprise you."

"He won't," she mutters, giving up the fight and leaning into me as I run kisses over her shoulder and up her neck.

"Who is it?"

"No one you know." She turns in my arms, throwing a leg either side of my own.

It's the middle of the night and a loud bang wakes me. I frown. The room is cloaked in darkness, and it takes me a second to realise I'm still at Luna's place. Sitting up, I feel beside me to find the space where Luna was now empty.

I grab my mobile and check the time. It's two in the morning. I hear Luna's hushed whispers and frown. *Who the hell could she be talking to at this hour?* I get out of bed and pull on my jeans.

I carefully open the bedroom door. The hallway is empty, but Luna's urgent whispers alarm me, so I move faster, heading toward the living room. "Please," she hisses, "come back later."

"I want what I'm fucking owed," spits a man's voice.

I shove the living room door open, and Luna spins to face me, her expression full of panic. I arch a brow at the man holding her wrist in a tight grip. "Go back to bed," says Luna, pleading me with her eyes.

"What's going on?" I demand to know.

"Nothing, just go back to bed."

"It doesn't look like nothing."

"You heard her, go back to bed. I'll return her when I'm finished," the guy says with a cruel grin.

I give a slight shrug. "Okay," I say, turning to walk away. When I turn back to him, slamming my fist into his face, it catches him by surprise. "As if," I spit, taking Luna's other arm so he can't pull her down with him. He releases her to cup his broken nose as his backside hits the floor. "Get the fuck out while you can," I bark, tugging Luna behind me.

"Really, Lu?" he asks, glaring at her.

"Grizz, what have you done?" she hisses, trying to get around me to go to him. "You'll make everything worse."

"Fuck worse. I told you, you're not whoring yourself out anymore," I snap, keeping her behind me.

"It's her fucking job," the man spits, pushing to his feet. "And she owes me."

"For what?" I ask.

"Drugs."

I turn to her, glaring angrily. "Drugs?" I hadn't checked her for track marks, mainly because she never looks high, but that would make sense as to why she doesn't want to stay at the clubhouse—Axel makes the girls test regular.

"So, if you don't mind, I need my fucking payment," he continues.

Luna doesn't hold my stare. Instead, she lowers her gaze to the floor. "You're a junky?"

When her eyes reach mine again, she looks sad. "I thought you knew me."

"I don't know you," I spit, "and right now, you remind me of my mum, and that's not a good thing."

She pulls from my grip and folds her arms over her chest. "Then maybe you should go."

I shake my head in disgust. "Yeah, maybe I should."

"I've got shit to do, so make it quick," the man snaps, reminding us both he's still in the room.

"You're coming too," I tell him, standing to one side so he can leave.

He rolls his eyes in irritation. "Fine." As he passes, he fixes her with a look of disdain. "The debt just tripled." And then he leaves.

"Great, thanks for that," she snaps, giving me a hard shove in the back.

"Oh, I'm sorry, I thought I was helping you," I yell.

"By pissing off the men I owe money to?"

"It was before I knew you were a junky."

"You don't know shit about me, clearly," she screams, and Ivy begins to cry in the bedroom. "Just leave."

"Is he going to come back?" I demand to know because he didn't look like the type to give up easily.

"Yes," she mutters, rubbing her hands over her tired face. "With his friends probably."

"What does that mean?"

"It means you just made my life ten times harder, Grizz. The debt will never be paid at this rate. He just tripled it."

"I'll pay the debt."

She gives an empty laugh. "It's not money he wants. And unless you're gonna offer him free blowjobs and sex on tap for the next six months, you can't fucking help me."

The thought angers me and I clench my jaw. "Get your bags packed."

"I told you, I'm not going to the clubhouse."

I grab her around the throat and push her against the wall, making sure my mouth is positioned close to her ear as I whisper in a low, threatening voice, "No other man is going to touch you, so pack your fucking bags because you're coming with me."

Luna doesn't speak to me the entire walk to the clubhouse, which suits me fine. I'm still reeling from hearing about her drug habit. It never occurred to me she could have a problem.

Axel is still awake, and he steps from his office as we walk through the main room. "Everything okay?" he asks, taking in the bags stacked on the pushchair and Ivy in my arms.

"She's staying here indefinitely," I tell him. "She needs to be enrolled in a drugs programme."

Luna takes Ivy from me. "I don't need a drugs programme."

"You're not being in charge of that kid when you're a fucking junky," I yell, taking us all by surprise. Ivy begins to wail, and I instantly feel bad.

Luna looks at me with eyes full of hatred. "I am not on drugs," she says clearly. "The debt isn't mine, it's my mother's." And she spins on her heel and heads up the stairs.

Axel watches her before turning back to me. "You wanna start at the beginning?"

"I wanna meet with the Kings. I need to know more about her brother and his scumbag friends."

He gives a nod. "Consider it done."

"And I need the brothers to stay the fuck away from Luna."

He arches a brow. "You claiming her?"

"No, but neither is anyone else."

He gives a knowing smile and goes back into his office. I head up the stairs to find Luna, but it doesn't take me long. She's in her old room cooing at Ivy, who is now wide awake.

"My room," I mutter.

"Not a chance."

"I don't trust you not to run, so my room now," I order.

She rolls her eyes and gathers Ivy in her arms. It's not the only reason I'm keeping her close—I don't want any of my brothers paying her a visit during the night. "Where the hell would I run to?" she asks, passing me. "You just fucked me over."

Axel and I each have our own floor. There are three rooms on mine. Obviously, the first is my own, but I stop at the door next to mine and push it open, pointing for her to go inside. I made sure it was painted and cleaned after the first time I offered for her to come back here.

Luna lingers in the doorway, eyeing the room suspiciously. It's a huge improvement on her old room here, which only had basic furniture. "You'll sleep in here," I tell her, giving a small push so she goes inside. I watch as she walks around the room, occasionally running her hand along the soft blankets folded on the end of the bed or the nice furniture.

"A Moses basket?" she asks, stopping at the fancy one I purchased.

I shrug. "The lady in the shop said it was the best."

"When did you do all this?" she asks. "This basket costs a fortune."

"Last week, just in case you needed a place."

Her eyes soften, and I see the anger leave her. "That's the kindest thing anyone's ever done for me."

I point to the door at the other side of the room. "That leads to a smaller room. When Ivy gets older, you can make it hers."

"You want me to stay here?"

I shrug. "You're just as much a part of this club as anyone here."

I hardly sleep, so hitting the gym works out well because I'm back early enough to force Lexi to come shopping with me.

When I stop the van outside the largest baby shop in the area, she frowns. "What are we doing here?" Then she turns her surprised gaze to me. "Oh my god, did you get your date pregnant already?"

I fain insult. "I'll have you know I haven't laid a finger on Danii . . . yet," I say with a wink. "This is for Ivy."

"Fable's kid?"

"Luna," I correct, getting out the van.

She follows. "Hold on, are you two a thing?"

I frown. "No. God, no, she's a club whore." I hate saying the words, and I instantly shudder because it's not how I feel at all. "But she reminds me of someone, and I know if she'd have had some help, a lot of things in my life would've been different."

"So, you want to help Luna?"

"Exactly."

We go inside and we're immediately met by the shop assistant, who smiles brightly. "Good morning, welcome to Lala Land. What can we help you with today?"

Lexi snort-laughs, glancing at me in amusement. I ignore her and turn back to the assistant. "We need a lot of stuff," I tell her.

Her eyes light up in a way that tells me she works commission. "Fabulous. How far along are you?" she asks Lexi, who almost baulks at the idea this lady thinks she's pregnant.

"Christ, I'm not with this guy," she says, laughing again.

"Try to look less disgusted," I say, shoulder-barging her. The shop assistant looks embarrassed as she stumbles over an apology. "The kid is a few weeks old, and I need a pushchair, one of those car seats, maybe a cot?" I frown while I think before turning to Lexi. "What else do new babies need?"

She shrugs. "I have no clue. You should've got Duchess to come."

"I'll take you through what you need," says the assistant, pulling out a notepad and small pencil.

"I bet you will," I mutter, following her.

We get back to the clubhouse with a van full of things I never knew a baby needed, and I instruct the prospects to take everything to the room I plan to kit out for Ivy. "Why are you doing this again?" asks Lexi. "You spent a ridiculous amount on a kid that's not yours."

I shrug. "She's cute. Besides, if I can help her to get a good start in life, it's one less broken person. And isn't this what you asked for?"

"I guess so," she says with a smile.

LUNA

I watch as Duchess rocks Ivy to sleep in her arms. "It's been a while since I held a baby," she muses.

Hands go over my eyes, and I jump in fright. "Relax," Grizz whispers in my ear, sending shivers down my spine. "It's just me. Duchess, can you watch Ivy? I need Luna for a minute."

"Of course."

"Stand," he tells me, and I follow his instruction. He uncovers my eyes and tips me over his shoulder. I let out a surprised scream, and he swats me on the backside before carrying me from the kitchen and up the stairs.

He dumps me on my feet outside my bedroom. "What are you up to?" I ask, unable to keep the smile from my face.

He grabs my hand and leads me into the room and through the door to Ivy's bedroom. It's no longer empty, and I gasp. "I did some shopping," he tells me.

I step farther into the room, running my hand over the beautiful white wood of the new cot. "This is gorgeous," I whisper.

He takes me by the shoulders and spins me towards the window, where there's an expensive pushchair. I know it's expensive because it's the one I fell in love with but knew I'd never be able to afford. "Grizz, this is all so . . ." Words fail me. "But why?"

He gives a shrug. "She deserves the best."

"Thank you. I mean, words don't seem enough, but I'm so grateful. You really shouldn't be spending all your money on us."

He smiles. "The little goblin needs this stuff, and while you're part of this club, she'll never go without."

His words warm my heart, and it's almost on the tip of my tongue to tell him the truth about Ivy, but Axel barges in carrying tins of paint. He places them down and looks around. "Fuck me, that sales assistant had your pants down."

"Well, Lexi was no fucking help, Pres, so I had to rely on the assistant to tell me what to get."

"Maybe you should stop borrowing my old lady and get your own," he suggests.

I feel my cheeks blush, so I move over to the window and stare out. Ivy would never have all this stuff if I hadn't come to the clubhouse. Maybe Grizz is right—being here and accepting help will work out better. "Luna, here're all the things you'll need in this box," says Grizz, pulling my attention back to him. "You'll be able to paint her a mural like the one you started in your flat." He places the box beside the paints. "We'll leave you to it."

When Lexi joins me an hour later, she stands back to admire the pencil outline I've begun on the wall. "This is amazing. I didn't know you could draw."

I offer a weak smile. Nobody in the club would know this sort of thing, but why would they? "We've never really had chance to talk," I say, and she looks a little guilty.

"Which is why I wanted the guys to get closer to the women," she explains. "They should understand you're all human and not just a quick shag." She looks around the room. "And clearly, it's working, right?"

"It is?" I ask.

"Grizz seems really taken with you and Ivy."

"With Ivy," I correct. "He's really fallen for her."

"She's a cutie, so I don't blame him. Would he even know about her if he hadn't started looking out for you? Would any of us know?"

I shake my head. I had no intention of telling anyone at the club about my personal life. It's one of the reasons I didn't speak—they couldn't ask questions and discover what a shambles my life actually is. "He told me you can make bread?"

I laugh. "Can't everyone?"

"Apparently not like you. His eyes lit up when he told me how amazing it was. 'The best he's ever tasted' were his exact words. Maybe you could make some for the opening of The Bar?"

"Opening?" I repeat. At one time, I knew everything that went down in this club. Now, I'm out of the loop.

"Yeah, he's been working on a bar. It opens tomorrow night."

"Oh, I didn't realise."

"Well, everyone's invited, so dig out something good to wear." She heads for the door. "Maybe it'll be the night Grizz falls madly in love with you."

I scoff. "I don't think that'll happen." But after she's gone, I smile wide. I don't exactly hate the idea, and it's not like I haven't pictured it since he's been hanging around. He keeps coming back and doing nice things like this. But he didn't mention the bar opening, which makes me think he doesn't want me there. I go back to drawing and decide that if he asks, I'll go, but if he doesn't, I'll stay away.

I spent the day painting the picture I'd drawn on Ivy's wall. Duchess insisted on keeping Ivy with her, so I didn't get her back until it was time for her bath. And now, Grizz is in here watching my every move like I haven't bathed my daughter a million times over. "How come she doesn't slip out your hand?" he asks with worry etched on his face.

I laugh. "Here, you do it," I say, waiting for him to replace my hand with his own. "See, she's not slippery like an eel."

He grins. "I guess."

"Hold out your hand," I tell him before squirting a small amount of baby shampoo onto it. I watch as he gently massages it into her hair. It's only ever been me doing the bedtime routine, and as he rinses her hair with so much care and love, my heart swells.

Once she's wrapped in a towel, he hands her to me. "I've got somewhere to be. I'll check in later?"

I shake my head, embarrassed I was getting carried away in my head. "You really don't have to. I'll probably get an early night anyway."

He gives a nod and kisses me on the forehead. "Sweet dreams."

CHAPTER 8

GRIZZ

We enter the bar that's mainly frequented by the Kings. Axel gives a nod to their President, Reaper, who's at the bar waiting for us. We head over, and Axel shakes hands, taking a seat. "It's been a while," says Reaper. "What can I do for you?"

Axel nods at me to continue. "There's a guy working for you, Nate."

"Nathaniel?" he asks, pulling out his mobile and bringing up a picture. I give a nod. "What about him?"

"What's his story?"

He gives a shrug. "He's a runner for us, covering that estate. Brings in a lot of money, owes me a lot more. Why?"

"So, if I was to end him, that wouldn't be helpful?" I ask with hope in my voice.

He gives a laugh. "What's he done?"

"He's a piece of shit. I'm helping his sister out, and he's got her paying his debts."

"How is she paying for them?"

"By fucking whoever he owes."

"Luna works at your whorehouse, no?" Reaper asks, arching a brow.

"So, you know her?" I ask.

He gives a nod. "We know her. She hung around here until you took her."

His words sink in, and I bristle. The Demons had taken some of Reaper's club girls when Axel first took over, saving us from having to look for new girls. Suddenly, I don't like the idea of him knowing Luna intimately. "You know she's got a kid?" I ask.

He gives a nod. "Yeah, surprising really, thought social would've been in to take it."

"She's a good mum," I mutter, annoyed he'd think different.

"In answer to your question, I need Nate. He owes me too much."

"Does he get Luna to pay his debts to you?" I snap, and the mood changes.

He sniggers. "I've been there, done that, several times. Lu knows I have no issues with her. He pays my debt by working for free."

"How much is the debt?" I ask.

"Five grand."

"I'll have it cleared by morning."

I can feel my own Pres staring at me in confusion as Reaper laughs. "You're paying his debt? You know he owes all over the damn city, you'll be bankrupt."

"Whatever happens to him once the debt is paid is none of your business, right?"

He gives a slight nod, and Axel slaps him on the back and says, "I'll be in touch."

We get outside, and Axel grabs my arm to stop me walking ahead. "I don't get it," he says, looking concerned.

"I don't like the guy," I spit. "He's a prick."

"If you like Luna, just say it."

"I don't," I snap. "Not like that. This is all your fault," I add, arching a brow. "You forced me to get involved, and now, I can't walk away."

"Because you like her," he says clearly, like he's trying to convince me.

"No, because I see my mum in her."

Axel's arm drops to his side, and now, his expression has changed to one of pity. I turn my back and head for my bike. "I don't need you analysing," I throw over my shoulder as I get on my bike.

It's late when we get back to the clubhouse, but I can't deny the buzz I get when I see Luna is still up. The fact Fletch is talking to her bothers me more than it should, so I head straight for the bar and grab a whiskey.

"So, you pay her debts," Axel begins as he takes the stool beside me.

"Not her debts," I bite back.

"So, you pay her family's debts. You move her in next to your room. You treat her kid like it's your own. Where's this ending, brother?" I remain silent because I have no idea. "Cos let me tell yah, if this is all cos you wanna rescue a damsel, fine. But if you're trying to ignore your feelings for her, that shit's gonna eat you away inside."

"I've got it under control."

"Really? You don't look like you do. You're sitting here all pissed cos she's talking to Fletch."

"I don't give a shit who she talks to," I snap.

"That little baby haul you got her cost a pretty penny, and now, you're just gonna give five grand away so you can end her brother? You heard what Reaper said, he's got debts all over the place. More people will come looking, then what? Are you gonna pay them all? Fight them all?"

"While she's here, she's safe."

"And what if she decides to leave?"

"She won't."

He scoffs. "You haven't thought this through. You're playing happy families with her for now, so she's happy sticking around, but if you're not interested in her like that, what's gonna happen when you bring someone back? What if you and that Danii work out?"

"Luna knows her place in this club," I tell him. "I asked the guys to lay off her while she looks after her newborn baby, not for any other reason."

"So, when she's ready, she can go back to fucking the brothers?"

I stand, annoyed he's quizzing me. I don't want to think about Luna with anyone else, but I don't tell him that. "Of course," I say firmly, making sure to look him in the eye. "She's a good fuck. And tomorrow, when you meet Danii at the opening, you'll see why Luna isn't on my radar like that."

I head upstairs to my room, get the five grand from my safe, and ride back to the same bar I just met Reaper in. I hand over the money, and he confirms the debt is paid. Nate is all mine.

When I get back to the clubhouse, Luna and Fletch have disappeared. Axel gives me a knowing smile, but I ignore him and walk casually to the stairs. He can't know how pissed I am, but the second I'm out of his view, I take the stairs two at a time and head right for her old room. If she was gonna fuck him, it would be there. When I find it empty, I'm even angrier, knowing that if I find them in her new room, with Ivy right there, I'll kill them both.

I shove her door open and it smacks back against the wall. Luna sits up in surprise, dropping the book she was reading, and Ivy wakes, screaming like an alarm. "Christ," hisses Luna, "where's the damn fire?"

I glance around her room casually while heading over to Ivy's basket and lifting her out. I like that she instantly calms against my chest. "If you're looking for Fletch, he isn't here," she says, narrowing her eyes.

"Did you two—" My words are cut off by her steely glare. "It's none of my business," I quickly say, even though I'm pleased.

"I don't know why you're so bothered who I spend my time with," she casually mutters, grabbing her book and opening it.

I lay Ivy back into her basket and cover her with a blanket. "Tell me about the debts."

She sighs heavily, placing the book on her bedside table. "Why?"

I shrug from my kutte and place it on the hook by the door. "You said you're paying your mum's and Nate's debts?"

I kick off my boots and slip from my jeans, throwing them over a chair before sliding into bed beside her. I don't plan on staying with her, but I want her to open up, so I wrap an arm around her and pull her to lay against my chest. When she throws her leg over mine, I run my other hand up and down her thigh. "After Dad left us, we realised he'd run up loads of gambling and drug debts. Mum was already selling herself. She'd worked on the streets. It's how she met Dad."

"He was a customer?" I ask.

"Yeah, and then he became her pimp. Anyway, after he left, there were always debt collectors at the door. They took whatever we had worth anything and it still wasn't enough.

Mum made a deal and sold herself to them. And there were a lot of men calling. Then Nate started working for some dealers. It got us some good money in and we'd almost paid the debts, until he started taking the gear. He'd take what little money Mum earned and spend it on drink and drugs. When I turned eleven, he said it was time I earned my keep." The words sound bitter, and I place a gentle kiss on her head. "You'd be surprised how many men pay to have sex with an underage girl."

"Sick fuckers," I mutter.

"And it's been the same thing ever since. I give them half my earnings from Zen, and they stay off my back. But lately, Nate's been getting in too deep. He owes the Kings money, and they want cash, so he's working for free right now to sell their gear. Which means he's turning to others to supply him, and those men are happy to exchange it for sex."

"Jesus, Luna. Why didn't you tell anyone this? Axel would've helped."

"Do you know how embarrassing it is to talk about this stuff? Family is meant to support and help, not use and abuse. I was coping fine until I had Ivy."

"You didn't tell any of us about her. You just stopped coming here." I pause before adding, "Yet the Kings know."

She bristles. "You spoke to someone there?"

"I spoke to Reaper himself."

She drags her leg from over mine and pushes to sit. "Why?"

"Club business. Why did he get to know but not us?"

"Because out of everyone in my life, the Demons are like my family," she snaps, "and I couldn't stand to be kicked out."

"Kicked out?" I repeat.

"What good is a club whore if she can't have sex?" She turns to look at me. "I'm not stupid, Grizz. I know we're not seen as part of the club and I get why, but to me, you were the closest thing to family. It hurt less for me to make a choice and walk away than be kicked out."

Her words are like a punch to the stomach, but she's right. Until Lexi came along to force us to take notice of the club girls, we would have treated her exactly like that and replaced her. "Things are different now."

"Why? Because Lex forced you all to pick a girl and show some interest?"

"You slept with Reaper," I say, and the words pull at the jealousy I'm trying to keep hidden. "Is he Ivy's dad?" She gives her head a shake but avoids my eyes. "Did he hurt you?"

"No. He was . . . nice."

Nice. Her response pisses me off. "If he was so nice, why did you come to the Demons?"

She rolls her eyes. "If you're gonna get all pissy about it, don't ask."

I take a fistful of her hair and gently pull her to lie down beside me. I stare down at her. "He was nice?" I ask, arching a brow. "I don't wanna know if he was nice."

She smirks. "Then don't ask."

"If he was so nice, why didn't he help you with the Nate situation?"

"I don't think he knew. Well, not everything. But, at the end of the day, he's a club president, he's not going to rescue a whore."

"Jesus, Luna, stop referring to yourself like that. Those days are behind you."

"No, Grizz. I'm taking a break, but let's not pretend those days are gone because, eventually, you'll get bored of babysitting me and your life will go on. But Ivy and I will still be stuck in this shitty life."

I don't want to think about that too much, so I kiss her. When I pull back, her cheeks are flushed pink. "Bread," I say, and she frowns. "Why don't you open up your own place and bake bread?"

She laughs. "It must be nice to be in there," she whispers, running her fingers through my beard and tapping my temple. "Your head is so full of wild ideas."

"It's a good idea," I defend.

"An impossible one. Do you think I'll get a business loan when I have no real address and no proof of income?"

LUNA

It feels different this time as Grizz slides into me. We're both completely naked, which is a first because sex with us is usually rushed or more urgent, resulting in only half our clothes being stripped. Tonight, he took time to remove each layer, placing soft, gentle kisses on my skin. And even now, as he fucks me slow, his face is buried into the crook of my neck and he occasionally kisses me there or on the mouth. I'm not used to this kind of sex. Not with anyone.

When I eventually come apart, he places a hand over my mouth so as not to wake Ivy, but he whispers obscene words in my ear, dragging out my orgasm. And when it's his turn to climax, he spins us so I'm on top but keeps his hands on my hips to make sure I continue to move slow. Our bodies are slick with sweat, and when he comes hard, I follow with a second orgasm.

And then he pulls me into his arms, only shifting to remove the condom and drop it in the bin beside the bed. We fall asleep wrapped in each other.

When the morning comes, I can't pretend I'm not disappointed to find his side of the bed empty again. There's no note, but then I guess he doesn't need to leave me one now. I already know I'll see him later, and I smile to myself at the thought.

Lexi is the only one in the kitchen when I get downstairs. She moves to pour me a coffee, insisting I sit. Ivy is snuggled in my arms, so I don't argue. "You look all . . ." she pauses before shrugging and adding, "glowy." I press my lips together to try and stop the huge smile from spreading, but she spots it immediately and takes her seat again, sliding the coffee in front of me. "Spill," she orders.

"I guess I'm just happy," I say.

"Because?" she pushes.

"I'm here, where I feel safe."

She reaches across and gives my hand a gentle squeeze. "You should never have left. Any idea what you want to do with your time once you're healed from Ivy?" I smile again, remembering what Grizz suggested last night, and I relay it to her. "That's not a bad idea," she tells me.

"It's a dream is what it is. How the hell would I get funding for it?"

"Ask Axel?"

I shake my head. There's no way I'm going to ask him for money. I've done my best to avoid him pretty much since I returned. "Maybe I'll find something in a supermarket if Duchess can help with childcare. Or a bar?"

"Speaking of bars, have you found an outfit for tonight's opening?"

"I'm not going," I tell her. "I don't have anyone to watch Ivy, and he hasn't mentioned it."

"He probably just forgot. I'll ask Duchess to babysit."

"No, she's done so much for me already, and I don't want to push into his life. When I say he hasn't mentioned it, I mean any of it, not even the bar."

"Luna, you are a part of this club and you are coming

tonight. All the girls are going. So, let's find you something to wear."

I've never been one for girly chats and sharing makeup. I never had the time as a teenager, and it didn't come naturally as an adult. I'd learned young to keep my life private to avoid people judging me, but something about Lexi and her demeanour has me spilling about last night with Grizz as she watches me apply my makeup.

"That sounds like you made love," she says, looking excited.

"Only when I woke, he was gone."

"These men are busy. Maybe he had shit to do with the bar to get ready for tonight."

I shrug. "He doesn't treat me like a whore," I admit. "It's nice."

"Maybe you just need to ask him. Talk to him tonight."

I shake my head. I'm already sick with nerves even though Lexi's spent the day trying to convince me he'll want me there and his lack of invite is purely an oversight. By the time we arrive with the other girls, I'm practically shaking.

Axel takes Lexi under his arm and kisses her on the head. When his eyes reach mine, he frowns. "Does Grizz know you're coming?"

It only unsettles me more, but Lexi laughs, grabbing my arm and tugging me toward the bar. "Ignore him, he's joking."

When I look back over my shoulder, I spot Axel looking around wildly and I can't help but think he wants to warn Grizz. And then my eyes land on him. He's wearing black—a long-sleeved black shirt with black jeans and his usual heavy boots. His kutte is firmly in place, and I can't help but admire how hot he looks.

I don't immediately see the woman he's hand-in-hand with, but as my eyes focus and my mind plays catchup, he looks my way and I realise Axel has spoken to him. I know there's devastation playing out on my face, but it's far too late to back out now and pretend I was never here. So, I take a deep breath and force a smile before turning back to Lexi, who is now holding two drinks.

"You okay?" she asks, frowning.

"Don't look but Grizz is here with someone."

Of course, her eyes search him out and her mouth falls open. "Oh fuck. I swear, I didn't know, Luna," she rushes to add.

"It's fine," I say, my voice coming out as a squeak.

She winces. "What do you want to do?"

"Just act normal."

"I mean, that's gonna be hard when you look like you want to cry."

I take a drink of the blue cocktail she handed me and cough. "Christ," I gasp, "what the hell is this?"

She laughs, patting me on the back. "Good cover. Now, you can say your eyes are watering because you choked on the blue monkey."

I join in her laughter, momentarily forgetting about Grizz.

CHAPTER 9

GRIZZ

"Why do I think you have something to do with this?" I growl close to Lexi's ear. She jumps before spinning to face me.

"You made love to her," she hisses, poking a finger to my chest.

I frown. "Huh?"

"You've been leading Luna on, and now, she's devastated."

I groan. "Is she?"

"Of course, she is, but don't you dare tell her I said that. What was last night about if you don't like her?"

"I do like her. She's a lovely girl."

"Oh god, that doesn't sound good."

"I'm not talking about this with you," I tell her, turning away to look for Danii. I let out a second groan when I see her speaking to Luna. "Fuck, she'd better not cause me trouble or I'm blaming you," I tell Lexi, stomping over to where they are.

Danii smiles wide, sliding her arm around my waist. "Here he is, the man of the hour."

Luna gives an awkward smile. "Congratulations."

"What are you two talking about?" I ask briskly, feeling Danii's eyes on me.

"I recognised Luna from the church," she tells me. "She helps out and makes the most amazing bread."

"Does she?" I mutter.

"Excuse me, I need some air," Luna almost whispers, walking away.

"Oh, that was odd," says Danii. "We were having a lovely chat until you came over. Don't you two get along?"

I shrug. "She's a club wh—" I stop the words because Danii wouldn't understand. "She hangs around the club. How do you know her from church? Are you a Christian?"

She shakes her head, laughing. "No. I donate whatever food is left from the coffee shop at the end of the day on Wednesdays."

Lexi comes over. "Danii, I need you to come and help decide what drink I should try next," she says, pulling her away. I take the hint and head outside to where Luna is scrolling on her mobile.

She looks up and immediately shoves her mobile away. "Lexi convinced me to come," she blurts.

I feel bad. I wanted to explain about the opening and invite her, but that meant I had to tell her about Danii, and I wasn't ready to see the hurt on her face. The hurt I'm witnessing now. "It's fine," I lie. "I just forgot to mention it."

She gives an unamused laugh. "I think we both know you didn't want me here."

"Luna," I say on a heavy sigh, "it's not as easy as I want it to be when it comes to me and you."

She pushes off the wall. "Me and you? I'm not an idiot, Grizz. I know there's no me and you."

"Really?" I ask, arching a brow.

"I'm a club whore. Brothers don't marry club whores and live happily ever after. They fuck them, and that's good with me." She looks past me to inside the bar. "She's pretty."

"So are you," I mutter, my heart aching inside my chest.

"She looks so . . ." She frowns like she's trying to think of the right word before adding, "Clean. She's perfect for you."

She goes to head inside, but I slam my arm across the door to stop her. "I wanted to tell you," I try to explain.

She ducks under my arm and steps inside, turning back briefly and asking, "I assume you won't be needing my services tonight?" She forces a smile. "I'll let the guys know I'm back in business." And then she's gone, pushing her way through the crowd and leaving me with any objection stuck in my throat.

Fletch and Kade, one of the prospects, are either side of Luna. They're buying her drinks and making her laugh and doing shit that makes me want to rip all my hard work apart in this bar.

"You okay?" asks Axel, slapping me hard on the back so I drag my eyes away from the threesome that's playing out in front of me. "You haven't taken your eyes off her."

"I thought you told the guys to stay away from her?"

He gives a nod. "I did. But we agreed it was only until she was happy to make a comeback. She's an adult and she can use her own words."

"She's not ready."

"Luna," Axel shouts, and I groan when she turns around. He signals for her to come over. "You need to hear it for yourself, VP," he mutters to me.

"It's Fable," she tells him, and I bristle at her words. Using her club name is her way of showing me she's back to old habits. That was the only word I needed to confirm it.

"My VP is concerned you're not ready to hang out with the brothers. Are Fletch and Kade bothering you?" he queries. She gives a shake of her head and does that small, shy smile she used to do when she was being Fable. I decide I hate it. "Just so we're clear, you don't have to do anything you don't want to. You're free to stay at the clubhouse for however long you need, rent-free, and you're not required to fuck anyone you don't want to." She gives another nod.

"Words, Luna," I growl. She brings her eyes to me, and this time, instead of seeing hurt, I see the Fable I used to know, the one who knew how to make a man fall to his knees. And with that comes silence. "I swear to fucking god," I warn, "you tell me with words or I beat the shit out of anyone who goes near you."

"I am ready to be a club whore again," she hisses through gritted teeth.

Her words hurt. Every single one is like a punch in the gut. "And Ivy?" I spit angrily.

"She was fine last night while you were fucking me." The words come so quickly, I don't have time to tell her to shut the fuck up. And now, Danii is standing behind her, glaring at me. She spins on her heel and marches out the bar.

"Fuckkkkk," I yell, rushing after her. "Danii, wait." I catch her wrist and pull her to stop outside. "It's not what you think."

"Really?" she asks, and now, her eyes are full of hurt. "I mean, I know it's only been a few dates and we haven't done any of that stuff yet, but I thought you liked me."

I lead her around the side of the bar and away from listening ears. "I do like you."

"But you're having sex with somebody else."

I scrub my hands over my face. "I was but not anymore."

"I don't care. I'm not hanging around to be cheated on."

"Luna doesn't mean anything to me," I lie. "Not like that."

"You're having sex with her," she snaps.

"That's her role," I mutter, knowing she won't understand before I've even completed the sentence. "She works at the club."

"As a prostitute?"

"Not exactly. There are women who hang out at the clubhouse to have sex with the brothers," I explain. "They get free food, and they get to live there rent-free."

"Not free—they have sex," she says.

"It's been that way forever. The women are well looked after, and I know it sounds shit when you don't live that life, but I promise they're never forced into anything and they're happy to live that way."

She takes a step back with a look of disgust on her face. "And if we became a thing, would you continue to have sex with her?" she demands.

LUNA

I hold my breath, waiting to hear Grizz's reply. I couldn't help but follow them out. A part of me wanted to reassure Danii that Grizz isn't a monster, even though my heart's in tatters. It's my own fault for getting carried away.

"No," he says firmly. "Luna is a club whore and nothing more. We have a good time together, but the second I get involved with someone, that stops."

"How do I know you won't go back to her? She looked upset back there, like she really likes you."

"Maybe she does. Maybe she's got things twisted. That happens sometimes. I'll have a word with her and make it clear. I like you, Danii. When I think of my future, you're the sort of woman I'm looking for. You and she are completely different, worlds apart."

I ball my fists in anger and force myself to flag down a cab. At least I know where I stand.

———

Grizz doesn't come and see me when he finally arrives back at the clubhouse. I hear him stumbling around, trying to unlock his door, but I don't bother to help him, not wanting to face him after overhearing his conversation.

The following morning, I head down for breakfast and almost stop in panic when I see him hunched over the worktop, resting his head on his arms. He's in his running gear and wet through with sweat. Lexi spots me, so I continue my path to the table and sit beside her. "Where the hell did you disappear to last night?" she asks.

"I needed my bed," I tell her. "I'm not used to partying anymore."

"I came looking for you," says Grizz, and I stiffen slightly at his words. "You just left without a word."

"I came looking for you," I tell him, keeping my back to him. "You were busy, so I grabbed a cab."

"I thought you'd left with Fletch and Kade."

I roll my eyes even though he can't see me. How the hell did I end up telling Axel I was fine going back to being a club girl? "Oh," says Lexi, frowning. "I thought you were taking a break from all that?"

"Nope, apparently not," says Grizz, and I feel him behind me. "She's back open for business." And then he leaves.

"What the hell's that about?" whispers Lexi. I shrug, blinking away the tears that have decided to gather on my lower lashes without permission. "Hey," she says, rubbing my arm, "you wanna talk?"

We go back up to my room, where Ivy is still fast asleep after her morning feed. "I overheard him with his new girlfriend last night," I tell her. "He basically told her she's the one for him and explained how I'm a nobody, just a club whore doing her duties." I groan, burying my head in my hands. "Why did I let my brain get so carried away?"

Lexi gives me a sympathetic smile. "I don't think I helped there, did I? I shouldn't have pushed you into coming last night. I just saw the way he spoke about you, and I felt there was something there."

I scoff. "You should've heard how he spoke about me last night. And the worst thing is, I can't even be mad, can I, because he's right. I'm just a whore, and he's a biker—I was doing what I'm supposed to do."

"Bullshit," she snaps. "He's got to take some responsibility in this too. He's been all over you and practically ordered everyone to stay away from you. It's giving claiming vibes."

I roll my eyes. "Clearly not. I'm such a twat."

The door opens and a freshly showered Grizz pops his head in. "Oh," he mutters upon seeing Lexi. She scowls, not bothering to move, which is clearly what he wants as he steps into the room. "Can we talk?"

"I think you've done enough talking," Lexi mutters.

"Of course," I say, giving Lexi a warning glare.

"Can you give us a minute, Lex?" he asks, and I desperately want to grab onto her to stop her leaving. She looks to me for confirmation, and I give a reluctant nod.

Once she's gone, he sits on the edge of my bed. "What's her problem?" I shrug. "I wanted to talk about last night."

"I shouldn't have come. I'm so sorry."

He goes to grab my hand, but I retract it, and he frowns. "What I was going to say was that I should've mentioned it. I made it weird by not. And I should've talked to you about Danii."

I'm already shaking my head. "You really don't need to apologise. What you do in your private life is nothing to do with me."

"But we're mates, right?" His words sting, but I give a nod. "So, I should've told you, and honestly, I don't know why I didn't."

"Glad we cleared that up," I say, pushing to stand. I just need him gone because the more he talks, the more my heart aches and the more stupid I feel. He grabs my hand, forcing me to stop beside him. His hand goes to my exposed thigh and he gently runs his thumb there. I hate the pity in his eyes, so I turn on the Fable charm and smile shyly, placing my hand on his shoulder. It's not what he was going for, and I can see him already wanting to pull away. He doesn't like me as Fable for some reason, so I play it to my advantage.

"Sorry, did you want some time alone?" I glance at Ivy before turning back to him. "I've probably got ten minutes before she wakes."

He arches a brow and stands, his hand falling from me. "No, Fable, that's not what I want," he mutters, and the use of my alter ego hurts.

I force another smile. "Okay, well, have a great day, and you know where I am if you need me." I turn away and busy myself with making the bed. I wait until I hear the door open and close before dropping down onto it and burying my face into the covers. *Fuck, I need to get my shit together.*

CHAPTER 10

GRIZZ

I've spent most of the day looking for Luna's brother, but as it gets closer to opening time at The Bar, I have to admit defeat and give it up. I'll try again tomorrow.

Axel asked me to hire a bar manager, but I haven't gotten around to it yet, and honestly, I enjoy hanging here. Taking up one of the booths nearest the bar so I'm on hand to help, I lay out my receipts. Cash gave me a crash course in bookkeeping, and although he'll do most of it, I've been tasked with listing my expenses.

I'm so lost in it that when Danii slides into the seat opposite me, I don't immediately notice. She clears her throat, bringing me from the numbers, and I smile. "Hey, what are you doing here?"

She glances at the bar, and I follow to see a group of women. "I thought I'd bring my friends here to sample the cocktail menu."

We'd parted last night on rocky terms. She'd allowed me to

walk her home, but a kiss was out of the question. Funnily enough, it made me want her more, and as she sits before me now, all dressed up nice, my cock twitches. "The first round is on me," I tell her.

"I thought about last night a lot."

"Okay."

"And I'd like to give it a go."

I'm surprised at her words. We didn't really discuss where we were headed and it's only been a few dates, so I lean closer. "Us?" I ask for clarification.

She gives a nod. "On one condition."

I smirk. "You're giving me conditions?"

"I've been hurt way too much to get to this age and let it happen again. So, take me to the clubhouse."

"Why?" I ask, frowning. One thing is for certain—I'd planned on keeping the two very separate.

"I want to see it for myself."

"It's an old factory with a bunch of bikers living together like a frat house. It's nothing special, trust me."

"Still, I need to see it for myself to understand it. You say these women hang around for sex, I need to see that."

My frown deepens. "You want to watch the women having sex?"

She blushes, laughing. "No, of course not. I just have to picture this place for myself because what I'm imagining is terrible."

I give a nod in understanding. It's Sunday night, so the clubhouse will be quiet, and it's probably the best time to take her. "Okay. I'm leaving here in an hour. You're welcome to come back with me."

I'd dropped Axel a text warning him I was bringing Danii back. I asked him to ensure the place wasn't in chaos, so when we walk into a full-scale party, I feel like hunting him down to punch him.

Smoke is at the bar, and I slap him on the back. "What's the celebration?" I ask, keeping our backs to Danii.

"Lexi started it," he says with a shrug. "She doesn't need an excuse lately." I roll my eyes. I wouldn't put it past her to have done it on purpose.

I hand Danii a vodka and Coke and down my double whiskey in one. Grabbing her hand, I lead her to the couches, pulling her onto my knee and trying to act as normal as possible, even though I'm nervous as fuck. This is most definitely gonna scare her off.

Her eyes scan the room in amazement. I forget how weird it must be for a newcomer to see all this. To us, it's everyday life. "Is it like this all the time?" she asks.

I shrug. "Sometimes. Usually, it's quiet in the week."

She grins. "It's crazy." Her eyes fix on something and her mouth drops open. "Oh my god, that woman is practically naked," she whispers, and I turn to see London dancing on the pool table in her underwear.

"There's a lot of that," I admit because I have no choice but to be honest. I wince before adding, "It often goes further."

Her eyes widen. "Like sex?"

I nod. "Sometimes. The guys get carried away and it can start in this room. I'm only telling you in case it happens tonight."

Her cheeks flush as she bites her lower lip. "Did you do that?" I briefly close my eyes before giving a quick nod. "Don't you feel . . . exposed?"

I laugh. "Not usually, but it's been a while since I did that shit."

Heels click against the floor and I glance to where Fable is walking across the room. She's dressed in a long, green lace jumpsuit. Underneath, she's wearing underwear, but it's all on show, and I clench my jaw in annoyance.

"Is it weird seeing a woman you've had sex with doing it with other men?"

Danii's question pulls my attention back to her. "Not really," I say, shrugging. "These are my brothers, and it's just sex."

"Would you share me?"

I almost choke. "No. Why would I share you?"

"Maybe that's your thing?"

I pull her closer and inhale the scent of her fresh shampoo. "There are rules here. If we wanted to spend the rest of our life together, I'd announce it to the club and you'd be known as my old lady," I tell her. "They become part of the club too, and none of the brothers can touch someone's old lady."

"And don't the other old ladies mind women walking around here naked?"

I laugh. "No, they're used to it. The single brothers need club girls to keep them grounded. Besides, there's only Lexi who's officially someone's old lady."

She looks around the room again, and I take the chance to discreetly check out what Luna is up to. I stiffen when I see her with Fletch. He's standing behind her with his arms wrapped around her waist and his chin rested atop her head. They look at ease together as he talks to Axel.

Lexi joins us. She seemed to hit it off with Danii last night, which is a relief. If this goes anywhere, I know she'll feel welcomed into the club. "I was just explaining club life to Danii," I tell her.

"Oh yeah? Things hotting up between you?" It's an odd question, and my expression must show it because she adds a laugh and moves on quickly. "You get used to the noise and the half-naked women strutting around."

"Doesn't it bother you that they're around your husband?"

Lexi shakes her head. "Nah, he knows where his bread is buttered. He also knows I'd chop off his nuts if he went near any of them." She leans closer. "The secret is to befriend the girls so they feel a loyalty towards you. That way, if your man tries shit on, they feel obliged to tell you."

I laugh. "Does Axel know about this?"

She looks over to where Axel is still talking to Fletch. "I didn't think that would be long," she mutters absent-mindedly.

"What's that?" I ask, knowing she's talking about Fletch.

"Fletch and Luna. He's been after her since she came back." She smiles dreamily. "Maybe he'll claim her and they'll live happily ever after." She's trying to get a rise from me, and her expression confirms that when she gives me a subtle smirk. "Lord knows she deserves it."

"Can that happen?" asks Danii.

"Yeah," Lexi replies. "Some of the bikers are a little too stuck-up and wouldn't be seen dead claiming a club whore. But some of them, the good ones, they see past it and want to offer the world."

I bristle at her words and the obvious dig at me. "You're talking shit," I mutter.

"Am I?" she queries, arching a brow. "Luna needs rescuing. She's had a shit life."

"Why?" asks Danii.

"We don't need to talk about this," I snap, glaring at Lexi.

Of course, she ignores me. "Most of these girls are in this life because they've faced some kind of trauma," Lexi continues. "Luna is no different. It's why I came up with a scheme to pair the men with the club girls, in the hope they'd feel like part of the club and protected."

Danii smiles. "That's so sweet."

I zone out, uninterested in Lexi's mission to save a whore, and take my eyes back to Luna, who is now sitting on Fletch's knee with her arms around his neck. His hands are running through her hair, but when he tries to pull her in for a kiss, she dodges him and kisses his neck instead. He rests his head back on the seat and closes his eyes as she trails her hands down his chest.

I tear my eyes away. "Who's watching Ivy?" I ask Lexi.

"She's asleep. Lu's got the baby monitor on."

I push to stand, lifting Danii from my lap. "I'll check on her," I mutter, stalking from the room.

LUNA

I lower to my knees and unfasten Fletch's belt. I don't want to be here, not to do this, and I internally give myself a pep talk. It's not like Fletch isn't hot—he is. His body is solid, and he's got all the makings of an alpha male. And he doesn't stink, which is a bonus. But he isn't Grizz.

I haven't seen Grizz all day and I hate it. I got so used to him being around, and now that he's not, I feel abandoned. It's the reason I didn't want him hanging around in the first place, especially for Ivy. *Imagine if she was older and had gotten attached.*

"I'm all for the tease," says Fletch, breaking my thoughts, "but seriously." He finishes opening his trousers and releases his cock. I stare at it, and my body aches. *Why did I have to go and try to make Grizz jealous?* This is why I'm back here on my knees, because I'm too fucking stubborn for my own good.

Fletch's hand goes into my hair as he guides me closer to his erection. "Enough." The word is barked from somewhere across the room and Fletch instantly releases my hair.

I turn to Grizz, who's glaring down at me with contempt.

"Get the fuck off the floor and sort out your kid," he spits angrily. Ivy is nestled against his chest, but I can see she's awake. The room is almost silent, and I can feel eyes on me as I push to stand. He grabs my upper arm like I'm some diseased rat and marches me out the room.

Once we're out of everyone's view, he releases me but shoves me to walk in front. We go upstairs and into my bedroom. "She was awake," he snaps, laying Ivy on the change table. "She needs changing," he adds angrily. I go to take over, but he slaps my hands away. "What kind of mother would rather be on her knees sucking dick than tending to her baby?" This time, he glares at me, and I wilt under the intensity.

"I had the monitor," I mutter feebly, feeling the sting of each word he spits. "I was keeping an eye on her."

"You were on your knees about to suck cock. I didn't see you checking the monitor."

"Why are you so mad?" I ask, folding my arms over my chest. "Ivy is fine. She wasn't crying and she's been fed."

He removes her nappy and points out the explosion in there. "She needed changing."

I hate the way he's judging me again. It makes me feel ten times worse. "What's this really about, Grizz?" I ask, allowing anger to chase away the shame. "Why are you even in here checking on Ivy?"

"Somebody's gotta watch out for her."

I attempt to take over again. This time, his hand goes around my neck, and I inhale sharply. It's not aggressive. His hold is loose, but it's enough to keep me back. He drags me closer until we're practically nose-to-nose. "I don't like it," he whispers, looking tormented. "I don't like the return of Fable. Get rid of her."

My chest heaves with excitement as his eyes meet mine. They're full of heat and the desire to kiss him is strong. "Grizz?" shouts out a voice, and he briefly closes his eyes before taking a step back. Whatever he'd just felt is gone, replaced by the stone-cold Grizz, the one who hates me.

"In here," he replies, shoving me away.

Danii enters the room and her eyes dart between us as he goes back to changing Ivy's bottom. "Lexi pointed me in the direction of your room. I hope that's okay," she says, smiling.

I sit on the bed and fiddle with the lace over my knee. "We were just discussing parenting tips," he spits, his tone sounding pissed again. I roll my eyes, and Danii spots it, smirking.

"She's cute," she comments. She's seen Ivy before in church. "I didn't know you were the father," she adds, and I resist the urge to roll them again.

"I'm not," he says firmly. "If I was, she wouldn't be around to fuck up her life." His words are like daggers as he hands Ivy back to me. Staring down at her innocent face, a tear leaves my eye and rolls down my cheek. "Take the fucking night off and be a mum to your baby," he adds, leaving the room with Danii.

CHAPTER 11

GRIZZ

"That was a little harsh," Danii says as I unlock my bedroom door and usher her inside.

"She's thick-skinned, she can take it," I mutter, but she's right, it was a shit thing to say and if I could take it back, I would. But it's too late. I let jealousy get the better of me.

I pull Danii into my arms and kiss her. Taking her face in my hands, I brush my thumbs over her cheeks as I angle her face enough for me to take the kiss deeper than we've ever taken it before. I feel her melt against me then I pull back slightly, smiling at the blush creeping along her cheeks.

She chews on her lower lip. "I want to," she glances at my bed, "but I need to know something."

"Anything," I murmur, gently kissing her nose.

"Is there anything between you and Luna, or Fable, or whatever she calls herself?"

"I told you already, no."

"It's just, you seem to really like her."

I groan, pulling away. "She reminds me of my mum," I admit, sitting on the bed. "In a weird way. She never got that break in life to give her a chance to be a good mum, and I see that for Luna. She's a trainwreck, and I tried to stop it, but sometimes, you can't control everything."

"You care about her?"

"I care about the kid. I want Luna to sort her shit out and be a good mum. I kitted out the baby room and brought her here to keep her safe, and still, she wants to self-destruct."

"I'm going to be honest, now," she says, sitting beside me. "I really like you and I can see how kind and thoughtful you are. But I have a gut feeling about you and her, and I'm terrified to put myself out there in case you break my heart."

She's giving me a get-out clause. I could walk away now and this whole mess would be a lot less complicated. But deep down, I know Luna will break me and I don't want to give her the opportunity, so I look Danii in the eyes and say, "I'll do whatever you need to make you see I'm not into her. It's you I want."

She runs her hands along the denim of her jeans. "Okay. Stay away from her."

My eyes widen. "What?"

"She's next door to your room, for god's sake, Grizz. You told me you've been sleeping with her and you want to rescue her, and she's right next door to your room. How can I relax knowing she's so accessible?"

"She's part of this club."

She gives a nod. "I know, which is why I'll understand if you decide to say no. I think we could have something special here, but I can't explore it when I have this gut feeling about the two of you." She stands and moves between my legs, placing her arms around my neck. "Don't we owe it to ourselves to see where this could lead?" She kisses me, and I groan into her mouth, grabbing her arse and gently squeezing. She giggles, and my heart warms.

There's a knock on the door. "Fuck off," I bark, pulling her to sit over me.

"VP, it's urgent. You've got visitors."

I frown, placing Danii on her feet and opening the door. Shooter lowers his voice. "A guy called Nate is at the gates, but he's brought company."

I grin. "Saves me hunting him down." I turn back to Danii. "Wait here," I order.

As I step out the clubhouse, Axel follows. "You want me to gather the brothers?" he asks, eyeing the group of men the other side of the gate.

"No. He's gonna do this one-on-one," I mutter, stalking towards him. "But have them stay by the doors so he can see my reach is much bigger."

"I hear you've been looking for me," Nate states as I get closer. He's trying to sound more important than he is. The reason he knows I've been looking for him is because I offered money to anyone who could get him to me, not because he's got people watching out for him.

I spot the young lad I'd spoken to this afternoon, and he steps forwards. I slide an envelope of cash through the bars of the gates, and he takes it, giving a nod and then rushing off.

"Open the gates," I tell Smoke, and as they begin to slide open, I smirk. "You brought your little gang," I say, my tone mocking. I glance back over my shoulder at the bikers gathering at the entrance to the clubhouse. "And if that's the way you wanna do this, I'm down."

The men beside him shift uncomfortably. They're still boys really, not one of them over the age of twenty, and we outnumber them at least three to one. "What did you want me for?" Nate asks.

"It's a warning really," I say, tipping my head to one side. "A polite one."

"Let me guess, this has something to do with that whore you're protecting."

"If you mean your sister, yes. Ain't it time you took responsibility for your own mess?"

"I don't know if you've heard, but that's how a pimp/whore relationship works. She fucks, I reap the rewards."

I scowl. "Like it's not bad enough you're pimping out your own sister, but you're using her to pay your debts. That's lower than low."

"Have you ever asked what she wants?" he snaps. "She's been fucking since she was a kid. That says a lot about a person."

I step closer, and he does the same. I want to end him, but there are too many witnesses, which I suspect is the reason he brought his gang. "It says she was neglected, groomed, and abused."

"Man, you don't see what she's like. She's hungry for it, always greedy when it comes to cock."

It takes one hit to the centre of his face to knock him on his arse, and I almost laugh out loud. "Get up," I order.

He spits blood to the side of him and pushes to his feet. "You're really gonna fight over a used-up pussy like that?"

"You need to stay the fuck away from her and call off your army of scumbags. I'll kill every fucker who touches her."

He wipes his bloodied nose on the back of his hand. "We'll see, biker. We'll see." He heads off with his bitches following, every one of them looking relieved.

"Is that the end of it?" asks Axel, appearing beside me.

"I hope so, Pres, cos Danii just gave me an ultimatum."

I take Danii home, promising her I'll be in touch once I've thought over her offer. We'd fooled around after the little interruption. It'd been a long fucking time since I did that sort of shit, and just thinking about the way she gasped when I stuck my hand in her knickers makes me hard.

Axel joins me at the bar when I return and gets us a bottle of whiskey and two glasses. "You gonna fill me in on that ultimatum?"

"She wants me to avoid Luna."

"Right, what's the problem with that?"

I shrug, waiting for him to top up my glass before knocking it back. "I mean, full on avoid her. I think she wants her out the club."

He scoffs. "First of all, Luna is part of the club, so that ain't gonna happen. Until Danii becomes something more, Luna stays."

"Tell me what to do," I say, sighing heavily.

"How can I when you won't admit how you feel for Luna?" He rolls his eyes in annoyance. "You like her. What's stopping you going for it?"

"Danii," I point out. "I like her, Pres, and she likes me too."

"So, what's the problem? Move Luna back to her old room and avoid her." The thought makes me ache. The idea of having her away from me is harder than it should be.

"It sounds sick when I say this, but Luna is like my mum, and at first, I wanted to help her better herself. But now, I want to be there to see her change. She's like an addiction."

"And what if she doesn't wanna change?"

"Who wants to fuck for a living, Pres?"

"London, Siren, Foxy . . . I have lots of girls who wanna fuck for a living, Grizz. You have the problem with that, not them. If they hated this life, they'd save their money from Zen and get the fuck out of here."

"She's different," I mutter.

"Different because you like her, Grizz," he snaps. "Fucking wake up."

"I can't be with her," I snap back. "The thought of all the men she's . . ." I trail off. "I hate knowing that most of my brothers have been inside her, okay. And who the fuck knows how many others. You heard Reaper—he's been there, and so has half his club."

"Do you know how many men Danii's slept with?"

"No, I haven't asked."

"But there could have been loads, right?"

"It's different," I say. "If I get with Luna, all my brothers will look at us together and know what it was like to fuck my old lady. I can't handle that."

"So, you're gonna let jealousy win?"

I give a nod. "Yes, I am. I can't spend my life wondering if every man she passes has fucked her. Do you know what that'll do to me? Just the thought makes me sick to my stomach."

Axel glances over my shoulder and his expression changes. "Fuck. Luna, wait," he calls, jumping off his stool. I spin too, watching as she marches towards the exit with Ivy in her old pushchair. "Go after her," Axel barks, shoving me. "She heard what you said."

I run after her, catching her as she's mid-march across the car park. "Is it too much to hope you didn't overhear that?" I ask, wincing.

"In the last twenty-four hours, I've heard so much from your mouth I wish I hadn't," she says coldly.

"What's that supposed to mean?"

She stops, spinning to face me. "I heard you last night with Danii. And I heard every word just now. And I shouldn't be mad because everything you said is true, but I'd be lying if I said I wasn't hurting."

"Look, I'm sorry. I can't help the way I feel."

She gives a stiff nod. "And I can't help my past." She continues on, walking through the gate.

"Where are you going?"

"Away from here," she mutters. "It was a mistake coming back."

I rush after her again. "You can't be serious."

"This makes it easier for you," she cries. "You're doing what Danii asked, getting rid of me."

"That's not what I want," I yell.

"It is," she snaps. "You're just too scared to say it out loud. Let me go, Grizz. You're relieved of your duties."

"It's not safe for you to be out here."

"I've been surviving on my own since I was a toddler," she says with a sad smile. "I'm good at it. Take care, Grizz, and I hope things go well with Danii."

"Please," I mutter.

She stops again, this time fixing me with an angry glare. "No, Grizz," she snaps. "Whatever we had is done. Goodbye." And she stomps off.

LUNA

"Name?" asks the woman behind the desk.

"Luna Carter," I say, trying to keep my voice low.

The job centre is packed out with people either talking to advisors, like me, or sitting waiting. It's one large open space, so everyone can hear the conversations. I gently rock the pushchair, praying Ivy stays sleeping.

"What experience have you got?"

"None, really," I mutter, glancing around. "I haven't done an awful lot."

She narrows her eyes. "What have you done since leaving school?"

I squeeze my eyes closed before leaning closer and whispering, "I'm a sex worker."

"Huh?" she asks, turning her head so she can hear me better.

"I'm a sex worker," I repeat.

She arches her brows in surprise. "Right. Well, we don't get anyone looking for that kind of thing here. Let's skip experience and come back to it. Skills?"

I bite my lip so I don't laugh, and she must realise around the same time as me because her cheeks colour with embarrassment. "Listen, I'm currently unemployed and I need help to feed my baby. Can you sort that out?"

"Are you still producing your own milk?" she asks.

"Well, yes, but I can't feed her."

"Have you got a medical professional who can back that?"

I frown. "No."

"We need a note from your midwife before we can offer formula vouchers. We also need to show you're actively looking for work before we can get to the benefit forms."

I sigh heavily. This whole process is about forms and waiting. I left the clubhouse yesterday and decided I'd try to sort myself out. But getting here took so much effort, and now, they're asking impossible questions. "Say I find a job, will I get help with childcare?"

"You might, depends on your income."

"So, if I get a job tomorrow, I won't get help right away with childcare costs?"

She almost laughs in my face. "Fill out the forms," she says, piling them in front of me. "It can take anywhere up to ten weeks to hear back."

I gasp. "Ten weeks?"

"We have a backlog," she says, shrugging. "From COVID."

"That was years ago," I utter, taking the forms.

"There's an emergency loan you can apply for, but you'll have to pull a ticket and wait," she says, looking across the room. "There're a lot of people waiting." I follow the direction of her stare and groan. There's at least thirty people.

"Forget it," I mutter, heading out.

I grab a pack of noodles on the way home and stop at Mum's. It's been a while since I've dropped her any food round, and even though she's never shown a maternal side, I have the urge to be around her when my heart is so smashed up.

Ivy begins to stir, so I lift her from the pushchair once we're inside. "Mum," I call out.

I find her sprawled out on the couch, naked and bruised. I cover her with a blanket and go through to the kitchen. It's a mess, and I groan at the sight of stacked-up takeaway boxes and leftover food on plates that's now hard or mouldy.

I give Ivy her bottle and settle her back into her pushchair before rolling up my sleeves and beginning to clean up. I wouldn't usually tidy Mum's flat, mainly because it'll only be in this state again within a week, but I need to occupy my mind.

It takes me a good hour to get it looking like a kitchen again. I boil the kettle and make Mum the noodles, realising she probably needs them more than I do, then I gently wake her. She pushes to sit, wrapping the sheet around herself. "Luna?" she mumbles groggily.

"I've got you some food," I say, placing the bowl on the table, "and I cleaned the kitchen."

"You haven't come to see me in ages," she says, grabbing the bowl and shovelling food into her mouth.

"Sorry. I had shit to deal with. Are you okay?"

She gives a slight shrug. "With you not being around, Nate's been sending a lot of people my way."

"Sorry," I mumble, feeling guilty.

"You look sad," she comments, and she raises her hand to my cheek like she's about to cup it, but she thinks better of it and lets it drop onto her lap.

"I did the one thing you always told me not to do," I mutter, keeping my eyes on the ground.

"You let one in," she says, and her voice is so gentle, it makes me want to cry.

"Stupid really," I tell her. "He turned out to be a prick, just like the rest."

I hear the door open and close, and Mum's eyes widen in alarm. "Not again," she whispers, and for the first time, I see a glimpse of the vulnerable woman she is.

Nate appears, and I take in his black eyes. "You're back," he spits.

"Just here to check on Mum."

Two of his friends appear behind him. "Where's your hero?"

"I'm just about to go back to him," I lie.

"She's lying," Mum rushes to say. "He dumped her."

I glare at her, and she gives a helpless shrug. "I can't take it anymore," she whispers.

"He finally saw you for what you are?" Nate smirks. "When did he dump you?"

"What does it matter?" I ask, standing. "I have to go."

I try to pass him, but he shakes his head, grabbing my arm. "You owe me."

"I don't owe shit."

He slaps me so hard, my eyes feel like they're about to explode. I grip my cheek as tears spring to my eyes. "When did he dump your whore arse?"

"Last night," I whisper, my voice coming out as a squeak.

Nate shoves me towards his friends. "Take her to her flat," he says, throwing a set of keys to one.

"No, Nate, I have Ivy with me," I rush to say, trying to shrug them off as they each grab one of my arms.

"Mum can watch her."

"She can't. She's not fit to," I protest.

"Make me repeat myself and I'll put the fucking kid down the rubbish shoot," he barks. "The quicker you do what you need to do, the quicker you'll be back to playing Mother Teresa."

CHAPTER 12

GRIZZ

Danii crawls over my naked body, licking her tongue over my muscled abs. My cock twitches, but it's not raging hard like it should be at having this beauty stripped down to her underwear.

She sits over me, making sure her pussy is level with my cock, and she gently rocks against me. "I've been waiting for this," she whispers, running her hands over her bra and pulling the straps down.

I give my head a shake, trying to clear the images of Luna. Cos since she left the clubhouse a week ago, she's completely filled my head. I grab Danii by the waist and switch us so I'm hovering over her. *Maybe I need control.* She giggles as I unclip the front clasp of her bra and her breasts spring free. I stare. *All I have to do is fuck her. If I fuck her, I'll stop thinking about Luna.*

I dip my head and take her nipple in my mouth. She gasps, arching her back, and I release it, noting my cock isn't hard enough. I move down her body, parting her legs and settling between them. She waits in anticipation, and I can smell her arousal. That alone should have me fucking hard, but it doesn't. I groan, pushing up off the bed to begin pacing her room. It's pink and girly, and weird for an adult, but I haven't questioned it.

"Everything okay?" she asks, pulling a sheet over her half-naked body.

"No," I mutter, rubbing my forehead. "I'm fucking this up."

"Maybe I've put too much pressure on you," she says, her voice wavering. It makes me feel like a bigger prick.

"It's not you." She rolls her eyes, and I wince at my choice of words. "It's really not, Danii. You're beautiful and I can't believe you wanna be with me. But, right now, I'm a fucking mess."

"Talk to me. I might be able to help."

I begin to dress as she watches with disappointment clear on her face. "I don't know if I fit here," I say, looking around the room. Last night, we had dinner at her parents again, and she introduced me to her cousins and aunts. It was a real family affair and it made me realise it's not for me. "And more importantly, I don't know if you fit into my world."

"You haven't given me a chance."

I nod. "I know. It's all on me. But I can't fuck you knowing I might not be as into this as you are."

"So, that's it? You're ending it without giving us a chance?"

I inhale then nod. "I guess I am. I'm so sorry."

I leave, hating the hurt on Danii's face. That's two women I've fucked over in a week, and I feel like a massive prick.

I head to the nearest bar. It's next door to The Zen Den and it's way too posh for me, but I need some peace and good whiskey and this place offers both.

By the time I get back to the clubhouse, I'm exhausted. Wanting someone while telling yourself you don't want them is hard work. So, when I step into the clubhouse and find Luna in the doorway looking frantic, my heart leaps in surprise.

She turns to me. "Thank god, I need your help."

My eyes travel over the parts of skin I can see. Her face, her neck, her arms . . . they're all covered in bruises. "What's wrong?"

"Social services took Ivy."

I frown as I process her words. "What? Why?"

"It doesn't matter. What matters is you need to go and get her back. You can't let them take her to a foster home."

"Me?"

"Yes. They'll give her to you."

"Why would they do that, Luna? What the fuck is going on?"

Axel steps from his office. "Everything good?"

"Ivy's been taken into care," I say, the words angering me. "Why did they take her, Luna?"

She grabs my arm and tears spill down her cheeks. "Please, Grizz, go and see this lady." She pushes a piece of paper into my hand. "First thing tomorrow."

"And say what?"

"That you're Ivy's dad and you can look after her."

LUNA

2 hours earlier...

Hours . . . it feels like hours since I was forced into my bedroom by Nate's 'friends'. After I returned last week, Nate's been extra hard on me. That first night, he must have told his friends to punish me because I've never been so messed up in my life.

And it's been a similar scenario all week.

And just when I thought it wouldn't get worse, he sent four of his friends. Four men in the space of an hour is way more than my body can handle, and as the last guy shoves me from him, I fall onto my mattress and curl into a ball.

"You're losing your touch," one sneers as he dresses. "Getting as beat up as your mum."

He's right, this last week away from Grizz has taken a toll. I'm tired and hungry, and the men coming to see me are relentless.

I wait a good five minutes to make sure they're gone before pulling on my dressing gown and going up to Mum's flat to get Ivy. Nate takes her each day and gives her over to my mum, and even though she despises kids and has no bond with Ivy, she agrees to watch her because it means she doesn't have to have sex with the men.

"Mum," I call out.

I stop in the doorway to the living room to find two police officers and a lady who has Ivy in her arms. Nate is next to Mum, who is passed out on the couch. He gives me a smirk. "Here she is. Told you she'd be back."

All eyes turn to me, and I pull the dressing gown tighter around myself. I can feel them judging me. "What's going on?"

"Luna Carter?" the woman asks, offering a friendly smile. I nod. "I'm Becki Alcott from Social Services."

My blood runs cold as I stare at Ivy safely wrapped in a blanket in this stranger's arms. "Okay," I whisper, fear gripping me.

"We were called today to run a welfare check on Ivy."

"By who?"

"It was anonymous," she says gently.

"Can I have her?" I ask, making a move towards her. The police officer steps between us and the seriousness of this situation hits me like a tonne of bricks. *They're going to take my baby.* "Why can't I have her?"

"Where have you been today?" Becki asks.

I glance at Nate, who's looking smug, and it crosses my mind that he's done this so I'll have nothing to hold me back. My tears begin to flow silently down my cheeks. "I left her with my mum," I whisper.

"Your brother tells me you work from your own flat upstairs. Can we see it?"

I give a slight nod. The flat is a mess, I haven't had time to clean up, and sometimes the men who come order food for themselves and leave their rubbish behind. But refusing these officials will make the judgement worse. It's only a little mess after all.

I lead them up to my flat, with Nate following. As we get inside, he pinches my upper arm hard. "Keep me out of it," he hisses.

I stop in the hall and push Ivy's bedroom door open. It's the only room I know is clean, and Becki smiles. "It's beautiful."

When I don't move farther, the police officer pushes me to one side and they go into the living room. I stand in the doorway and take in the scene. Empty food cartons are stacked and there're ashtrays overspilling onto the table. There're two dirty bottles of Ivy's next to them, and the police officer begins to snap photos.

"What are you doing?" I demand, trying to pull his arm.

The other officer pushes me back. "You need to remain calm or you'll be coming with us," he warns.

I watch as he moves things from the table to reveal more mess. He lifts a glass coaster and takes a picture of the powdery residue. "That's not mine," I argue. "I don't do drugs."

Becki gives a smile that says she doesn't believe me. "Where does Ivy sleep?" she asks. "In her room?"

I shake my head. "Mine," I mutter. They head that way, and I don't bother to follow because I already know it's a state. There are at least three empty vodka bottles along with sex toys on the bed, and the sheets are a mess. I didn't see the point in washing them when there are so many visitors.

When they return, they're wearing grave expressions on their faces. "Is there anyone other than your mother who looks after Ivy?" I shake my head. "You have sole custody?" I nod. "In that case, we'll be taking Ivy into care today under the Child Protection Act. We will also be applying to the courts to ask for an emergency care order to be put into place. We're doing this because we believe Ivy to be at significant risk of harm and neglect." I sob, sickness filling my stomach. "I'll call to let you know when the hearing will take place, but they're usually in front of a judge pretty fast, so make sure you answer my call and get yourself some representation."

"What . . . I don't understand," I cry, her words feeling jumbled.

"Give me your telephone number and we'll be in touch. It's important you attend the court hearing. In the meantime, if you think of anyone who can take care of Ivy, let us know. We'll consider immediate family."

Present time

Grizz stares at me, and there's a storm brewing, I can see it in the way he balls his fists by his sides and his eyes narrow. "What did you just say?" It's spoken in a low, menacing voice, one I'm sure I should be terrified of, but since they took my baby, I have nothing left, especially not fear.

I wipe my face with shaky hands. "I was scared you'd run a mile," I explain. My entire body joins my hands, shaking so hard, my teeth clash together. "I thought you'd hate me."

"But we didn't... we never had unprotected sex."

I glance around and note Axel is now joined by a few of the other brothers. Humiliation courses through me. "Don't look at them," Grizz barks, causing me to jump at the tone of his voice. "Look at me."

I raise my eyes to his. "When you got out," I whisper.

He grabs my upper arm and shoves me towards the office. Axel steps to one side. "You gonna stay calm?" he asks Grizz, who gives a slight nod. "I'm right out here," he warns, closing the office door so we're alone.

"You're hurting me," I whisper.

He shoves me away from him like the trash he thinks I am. "I always use protection," he spits.

"We did at first, but you woke in the night and I didn't realise."

"You didn't notice I was fucking bareback?" he shouts angrily. "I was clearly hammered, Luna. Why the hell didn't you stop me?"

"I didn't realise."

"You did it on purpose," he yells, slamming his hands against the desk.

I shake my head. "I'd never do that."

He takes a deep breath. "Okay, so when you realised, why didn't you take care of it?"

"I meant to," I say, a fresh round of tears flowing. "I was busy at Zen, and my brother was on my back. I just got in a mess. I thought it'd be okay."

"Why didn't you get rid of it?" he shouts.

"Because I didn't find out until I was too far gone. Look, I just need you to get her back for me," I cry. "Ivy can't go into care. I'll never get her back if that happens."

He moves close, pushing his face into mine until my back hits the wall. "Oh, I'll get her back," he says, and I relax slightly, "but you're not going near her." His words are like ice, and I stare into his cold eyes. "You're not fit to be her mother."

"Grizz," I whisper.

"Tell me why they took her," he demands, stepping away and pacing the office. "Cos they don't do that lightly."

"Mum wasn't looking after her," I say.

"Your mum?" I nod. "The prostitute junky?"

"She agreed to watch her for an hour."

"And what were you doing?" I look at the ground. "What. Were. You. Doing?" He's back in my face, anger radiating from him.

"Working," I whisper.

"For your brother?" I give a nod.

His fist smashes into the wall right beside my head. I duck, covering my head and squeezing my eyes closed. I knew he'd react badly, but I'd hoped he'd be more concerned about Ivy than what I kept from him. Axel charges in and puts himself between us. "Relax," he warns.

"Get her out of my sight," Grizz yells, stalking towards the window and keeping his back to me.

Axel gently guides me from the office and closes the door. "What's he need to do to get Ivy back?" he asks. His sympathy causes my tears to flow faster until I'm gulping in air. "Focus," he says firmly as Lexi comes over with a tissue.

I reach into my pocket and pull out my copy of the social worker's details. "He should contact her. She has all the details of the court hearing."

"Court?" he repeats, frowning.

"It's procedure," Lexi explains. "A judge has the final say on Ivy's future."

"Will he let me have her back?" I ask.

She gives my arm a rub. "No, sweety. They don't remove children from their mother lightly. A judge will consider what's best for Ivy. If I was you, I'd get on board with whatever they suggest you do to be seen as fit again. It's not going to be a quick fix. You'll have a lot of hoops to jump through and some changes to make."

"I'll do anything," I whisper.

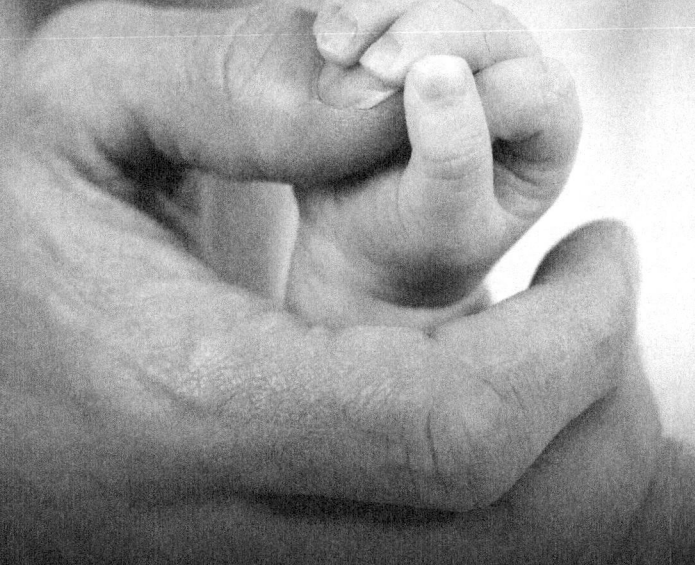

CHAPTER 13

GRIZZ

Axel comes back into the office, locking the door and closing the blind so no one from the club can see in. "Get your shit together," he orders.

"Easy for you to say," I mutter.

"You love that little kid anyway. This is good news, right?"

"I have a kid with a fucking slag," I yell, turning on him.

He squares his shoulders, daring me to follow through but knowing I won't. I turn back to look out the window. "You love her, Grizz. Don't try to convince me otherwise."

"It doesn't matter anymore. She lied to me. Whatever was there is gone."

"Bullshit. No one can turn off feelings that quickly. She fucked up, man. It happens. Help her get Ivy back."

I turn to face him again. "No."

"You're gonna let your kid go into care?"

"Of course not. I'll get Ivy back, but not for Luna. She's gonna stay the fuck away."

There's a knock on the door and Axel unlocks it to let Lexi in. "She's gone home," she tells us, locking the door behind her. "You okay?"

"Fucking amazing," I spit, and she arches a brow in that way a teacher would if you're out of line. "No, I'm not," I add, more calmly this time.

"It's a shock, but you don't have time to dwell on the past. What are we doing to get Ivy back?"

"Apparently, he's going to get her back and raise her alone," says Axel sarcastically.

"What about Luna?" asks Lexi, frowning.

"You want me to let her back into Ivy's life after she's let her down so badly?"

"Yes," Lexi says simply. "You know she's a good mum."

"Really? She's a prostitute, Lex."

"That doesn't make her a bad mum."

"But leaving her with a junky while she goes to fuck men does."

"It wasn't her finest hour, but she made a mistake—"

"It cost her child, Lexi. Stop making excuses. She had one job, to raise her kid right and keep her safe, and she failed."

Lexi narrows her eyes and places her hands on her hips. "You never made a mistake, Grizz? What's it like being so perfect?"

"I'd never let my kid down," I mutter.

"You already did," she yells, taking me and Axel by surprise. "She didn't get pregnant alone."

"I was drunk," I argue.

"That's not a fucking excuse," she snaps. "This is my whole point," she rants. "You all treat those women like personal sex slaves. They're humans, with lives outside of this club. They've suffered trauma and loss, and they're healing from scars, mainly caused by men. But none of you care about that as long as they can fuck. Well, it backfired, Grizz, and now, it's your turn to step up and fix this."

"I already said I'll get Ivy back, but I won't let Luna fuck her up."

"Aren't you the big man," she says, her voice dripping in sarcasm. "You're quite happy to break her heart and watch her fall, and now she's down there, you'll swoop in and rescue the baby you made together. What a fucking hero."

"Lexi," Axel mutters in warning.

"She loves Ivy and she was trying hard to change things so she could be a better mum. You didn't help in any of that," she says, shoving me in my chest. I arch a brow, glaring at Axel and willing him to get his woman under control. He gives a shrug, like he's waiting to see how it all pans out. "You gave her hope, Grizz, and then you dropped her like she meant nothing. You played a part in her fall, so don't stand there like you're fucking perfect. You're far from it."

Axel lets out a long breath as she steps back from me. "Now that's been said, you'd better call the social worker." He hands me a piece of paper.

Becki Alcott answers on the second ring. "My name is Warren Bear. I believe you took my daughter, Ivy Carter, into the care of the local authority today."

"Hey, yes, that's correct. How is Luna holding up?"

"I haven't called to talk about her," I say coldly. "What do I do to get Ivy back?"

There's a slight pause on her end before she recovers. "Have you been a part of Ivy's life for long?"

"Yes . . . sort of. I didn't know she was my daughter until now, but I've been in her life since she was two weeks old."

"Is Luna with you right now?"

"No."

"It would be helpful if you're on Ivy's birth certificate. The court will require a DNA test."

"I'll get that done."

"Ivy is under police protection for the next seventy-two hours. During that time, they can release Ivy into the custody of a parent, or it'll be put before a judge and an interim care order will be put into place. We'd prefer to work with the parents to keep your family together."

"So, what do I need to do?"

"I can come out and visit you in your home this evening?"

"Great." I reel off the address and set a time to meet.

I hang up, and Lexi fixes me with a hard stare. "Okay, this place needs a clean and, Axel, get all the things together that show what this club does for the community, every charity you've helped, and your plans for the future. They need to see this club as a pilar of the community and not a criminal gang."

"And if that doesn't work?" I ask.

"You'll need a safe place to live with Ivy. Go and find Luna. She was heading back to her place. I'll come."

"No," I say firmly. "I need to see her alone."

She glances at Axel for the final decision. He gives a nod, and I head out before he changes his mind.

———

Luna is sleeping. *She's fucking sleeping!* I slam her bedroom door open, and she sits up, looking around dazed. I pick up the empty wine bottle lying beside her and throw it across the room. It smashes against the wall, spraying tiny pieces in every direction. She ducks, a small scream escaping her.

I know why the front door is unlocked—it's so punters can turn up. She had my daughter here, in a flat where she'd left the front door unlocked for men to turn up to fuck. The thought makes me sick.

"Get up and shower. Now."

"Grizz," she mutters, scrubbing her hands over her face.

I head into the living room, frowning when I see the state of the place. Moving to the coffee table, I lift a half-drunk bottle of Ivy's milk. The teat is covered in ash from the nearby ashtray. *No wonder social took Ivy if they saw this shitshow.* I hear her approach. "Grizz, what are you doing here?" I don't miss the way her voice trembles in fear.

"This is where she's been living?" I ask, turning my angry gaze to her. She shrinks back slightly and folds her arms over her chest. "You let her live in this fucking shithole?" I yell, swiping my arm through the stacked takeaway boxes and empty vodka bottles. The mess sprays across the room.

"Things have been hard," she cries.

I close the gap between us until she's backed up against the door. "Don't you dare fucking cry again. If you'd have told me the truth, this wouldn't have happened."

"If you'd told me the truth, I wouldn't have got into this mess," she screams, shoving me away. I stumble back a couple steps. "You think I wanted this for her?" She waves her arms around at the mess. "I became exactly what you said . . . your *mother.*" She spits the final word like there's a bad taste in her mouth. "And I hate myself for it."

"I didn't make promises," I argue.

"But you made me feel seen," she cries, letting her hands drop to her sides like she's defeated. "For the first time, I felt wanted." My heart twists a little as I fight the urge to hold her. "And then in the end, when you got bored, you wasted no time reminding me what I was—a whore."

The front door opens and Nate waltzes in like he's not got a care in the world. Behind him is an older man who looks higher than a kite. Nate's eyes settle on me and he looks mildly annoyed. "You're back so soon," he comments.

"Nasty black eyes you got there," I tell him.

"Luna, are you ready?" he asks, ignoring me.

"Not now, Nate," she mutters.

"Look, unless you're paying, get the fuck out," he tells me.

I grin. "I warned you what would happen if you didn't stay away from her."

"You two are done, take the fucking hint."

"And I bet that suits you," I snap.

"What the fuck do you want with her anyway? She's a whore, and you've got a club full of them. What makes this one so damn special?"

I close the distance in two steps, smirking at the flicker of fear in his eyes. I look past him to the old fucker who's about shitting himself. "Get out," I tell him, and he wastes no time escaping.

Nate uses my short break in eye contact to pull out a blade. I catch the glint of the metal, but not quick enough to avoid the tip slashing across my stomach as he waves it around wildly. I take a few steps back, and Luna notices the knife. She jumps in front of me, screaming at Nate to stop. "I'm sick of him sticking his nose in our business," he snaps. "Move out the goddamn way or you'll be joining him."

I pull her back behind me. "Touch her and I'll break your fucking neck," I warn.

He begins to walk backwards until he's stepping out the flat. I let him . . . his time will come. "You have no idea who you're messing with," he says, grinning, before disappearing.

"Pack another bag," I tell Luna. "You can't stay here."

LUNA

Grizz doesn't put me on the back of his bike to take me back to the clubhouse. Instead, he calls a prospect to come in a car and drive me back. It's another subtle reminder that he doesn't want me around.

I keep my head bowed as I walk through the club. The

main room falls silent the second I step in, and I can't face the disgusted expressions now they know I've had my child removed because I couldn't keep her safe.

Grizz leads me upstairs to my old room, not the one beside his that I once shared with Ivy but the one on the whore floor. He slings my bag onto the unmade bed. "Shower and change. Wear something... appropriate."

"What for?"

"A meeting," he mutters, leaving the room without looking in my direction.

I shower and wash my hair, then I sit in front of the mirror and stare at my reflection. In the last week or so, I've changed. I look tired and sick. My pale skin is practically grey in colour, and the dark circles under my eyes aren't helping. If I had any tears left, I'd probably cry, but there are none.

I reach for the makeup bag I used to use and retrieve a bottle of foundation. I drop it back because I can't face applying it when I feel so empty. The door swings open, taking me by surprise, and Grizz stares at my naked body. "Was I not clear enough?" he asks. "We're leaving in five. Get ready."

I jump up, grabbing underwear from my drawer and pulling it on. His eyes aren't filled with heat like they used to be. Instead, they're full of hatred and anger.

I slip into jeans and a sweater and push my feet into the same old tatty trainers I always wear. His eyes linger there for a second before he grabs my leather jacket and throws it towards me. I catch it and put it on, then follow him out the door while tying my wet hair into a messy bun.

We use the car again, and he drives us into town, parking at the registry office. "Why are we here?" I ask, staring out the window at the people all rushing around after finishing work.

"You're putting me on the birth certificate."

I frown. "We can't just do that. We have to have an appointment."

"I know a guy," he mutters, getting out the car.

I sigh heavily and follow. He's already entering the building before I've even mounted the steps. I rush to catch up, but each stride he takes is worth two of mine. It's clear he doesn't want to be seen with me, so I slow my pace. When he stops at the reception desk, I hold back, not feeling worthy enough to stand beside him.

The receptionist leads us through to a grand office, where a gentleman sits behind a huge desk. He shakes hands with Grizz and tells us to take a seat, which we do. Grizz holds out Ivy's birth certificate, and I frown, wondering where he found it. He must have gone through my things at the flat.

"I need the full certificate, with my name on it," Grizz tells him.

The man gives a nod and begins tapping away on the computer. "Are you married?" he asks.

Grizz gives an unamused laugh. "No."

"Okay, let me just check the details. Ivy Carter?"

"That needs changing too," says Grizz, and I glare at his side profile. "Ivy Bear." I almost laugh at the name.

"Okay. And you're the mother?" asks the registrar, and I give a nod. "Can you confirm your name?"

"Luna Carter," I mutter.

"Okay. I'm adding Warren as Ivy's father, correct?" I glance at Grizz, realising I never knew his full name, which seems silly seeing as we've spent so much time together.

"Yes," I whisper.

He taps away on the computer before giving a nod. "All done." He prints the certificate off, and Grizz slides an envelope across the desk which I assume is full of cash.

We get outside, and he tucks the new birth certificate into his inside pocket. "I thought you'd want a test," I mutter.

"Oh, I do," he says, descending the steps and still not meeting my eyes. "But my name stays regardless."

"She is yours, Grizz. I swear it."

He ignores me, passing the car and heading into the town centre. "Where are we going?" I ask, trying to keep up with him.

"You need trainers."

"I can't afford—"

"I know," he mutters, continuing to speed walk in front.

The sales assistant in the sports shop is kitted out in tight Lycra shorts and a low-cut top that pushes her breast up in a way I can only dream of since having Ivy. She instantly flirts with Grizz, and he does nothing to deter her as they discuss which trainers they have in my size without asking my opinion. Not that I have one. Shopping is low on my list of priorities right now.

Grizz goes off with her, and I take a seat, staring down at the floor, my mind filled with thoughts of Ivy. When he returns, he holds out an open box containing a pair of white trainers. They look expensive, and the sort I'd always avoid. "Try them on," he orders. The sales assistant stands behind him, watching the exchange with curiosity. When I make no move to take them, he sighs impatiently and kneels before me. He removes a tatty trainer that looks so out of place in this shiny shop and discards it. He gently takes my ankle and slides the trainer onto my foot then proceeds to feel for my big toe, like I'm a child. It's so sweet, I almost smile, but then I remember he does this sort of shit and it means nothing. He hates me, and he wants to take Ivy from me.

He sets about removing my other trainer and replacing it with the new one. He then puts the tatty trainers in the box and stands. "We'll take these and the same pair in black." Then he goes off to pay, leaving me sitting on the chair wondering what the hell his game is.

When he drags me to the nearest clothes store, I stop. "Okay, what's going on?"

He gives me an irritated look. "You need new clothes."

"Why?"

"Because . . . because your shit is old." I'm insulted. I don't have money to throw away on clothes, sure, but what I wear isn't exactly falling off me. I always try to look presentable, and most of my time is spent in underwear because of my job. "Don't you want the social worker to see you're trying?" he asks. His words have the desired affect, and I trail behind him around the shop but not showing any interest as he grabs things and piles them into his arms.

By the time we get back to the clubhouse, I'm exhausted, but Grizz hasn't finished with me as he marches me to my room and picks out an outfit of designer jeans and a cream knitted top. I eye the garments. "The social worker is coming here in the next ten minutes. Get changed."

My eyes widen. "What?"

"You heard. Get changed." He stomps from the room, and I lower onto the bed and stare at the ground. The last twenty-four hours have been a lot to process, and the thought of now speaking to this woman who's messed my life up makes me sick to my stomach.

CHAPTER 14

GRIZZ

Lexi convinced me that having Luna in the meeting today would show solidarity, but I'm not so sure as I shake hands with Becki. She's smiling in an unsure way that tells me she's nervous about being here. I offer her a drink and try to put her at ease, but I'm sure being in a biker club was not on her bucket list.

Luna is already seated in the office and she looks sick with nerves, but at least she looks a little less of a mess. She offers a shaky hand to Becki, who takes it and lowers into the seat beside her. "How are you?" she asks.

"Not great," Luna mutters. "How's Ivy?" Her eyes light up whenever she says her daughter's name, which angers me more. She has no right to act as though she loves her when she's let her down.

"She's absolutely fine. She went into temporary emergency foster care. The family is very experienced with babies, so she's in good hands. Are you living here?" Becki asks, pulling out a notepad. Thinking of Ivy with strangers makes my mood worse.

Luna looks at me for instruction. "No," I reply for her. "She's staying here until she's back on her feet."

"Okay. And what does that look like, Luna?" she asks.

Again, Luna looks unsure, so I clear my throat. "A good job. Paying bills. Providing for Ivy."

Becki smiles at me. "If you could let Luna answer?"

Luna knots her fingers together nervously. "She's a selective mute," I say.

This gets Luna's attention and she frowns before sitting up straighter. "I want to get a job," she begins. "I tried, but it's hard when you've not had much experience anywhere."

"That's a good start," Becki says with a smile, making a note in her pad. "I can get you some support for that."

"I'll get her a job," I cut in before Luna can respond. She closes her mouth and folds her arms over her chest in a way that reminds me of a sulky teenager.

Becki closes her notepad. "Can you show me where Ivy will be sleeping?"

We head upstairs, and when I open Ivy's bedroom door, Becki smiles wide. "This is beautiful."

"She'll be in my room," I tell her, opening the conjoining door to the room where Luna once slept and pointing to the Moses basket beside the bed. "Until she's old enough to sleep in her own room."

"Perfect," says Becki, and she takes a deep breath. "Ivy can come and stay here. We can release her into your care," she says, looking directly at me. "And although we're more than happy that Luna will be a part of Ivy's life, for now, that will have to remain under the guidance of yourself and social services."

"What does that mean?" asks Luna.

Becki gives her another sympathetic smile. "You won't be able to be alone with Ivy for long periods of time."

Luna chokes on a sob and tears form in her eyes. "I'd never hurt her."

"No one is saying that," Becki rushes to reassure her, "but it's clear that you weren't coping on your own. It's great to see you now have support, and eventually, I'm certain you'll get back to where you were. So, the conditions of Ivy being able to come here is that Luna is not left alone with her for more than an hour at a time. There will be drop-ins from either myself or another social worker in the area. We'll do regular checks to make sure you're meeting Ivy's needs."

"How long will this last?" I ask.

"Until we're happy things are on track."

"When will she be home?" asks Luna.

"Tomorrow."

Axel calls church, and once we're all in, he explains to the guys the situation with Luna, also warning them to stay away from her. She's vulnerable right now, according to him, but I don't see it that way.

"And that brings me to her brother."

I bristle at those words. "That fucker is gonna die. He's the reason Ivy got taken into care. I think he thought having her out the way would make Luna more compliant as she'd have nothing else left. He's had two run-ins with me now, once outside the clubhouse and the other in front of Luna. It meant I couldn't end the fucker."

"You know it don't work like that, Grizz," says Axel. "We gotta vote."

"Is he a threat to the club?" asks Cash.

Axel shakes his head. "Not yet."

"He pulled a knife on me," I say. I'd kept it from Axel because I felt like a fucking pussy letting him walk away, but I couldn't end him in front of Luna and give her something to hold over me. I explain just as much when he fixes me with a quizzical glare. "I don't think he'll be happy I'm holding his sister here either."

"Why are we holding her here exactly?" asks Fletch.

"You don't care about her safety, Fletch?" I ask, arching a brow. "You seemed so keen to get in her knickers."

"Cos she's a club whore, man."

I growl, reaching for him, but Axel stops me, slamming me back into my chair. "We're not turning on one another over a woman. Especially one no one has claimed." He fixes me with a stare, and I back down. "I know you're not gonna like what I have to say, brother, but taking out Nate isn't on the list of priorities. We need you here, not back inside over some fucker just cos you don't like him."

"It's more than that," I snap, annoyed he'd think it's over a simple grudge. "He's pimping Luna out, and wasn't this whole bullshit experiment so that we treat the women more like family?"

"VP, I was tryin' to keep my woman happy. And maybe I hoped one of the women was the reason the coppers were still watching us, but nothing came to light, which means we go back to business as usual."

I stand. "I'm sure Lexi will be thrilled." I storm from the office, crashing right into Lexi. I steady her and mutter, "Sorry."

She smiles. "Where's the fire?"

"Did you know Pres is pulling the men off club girl watch? All that bullshit about treating them like family was crap to keep you happy."

She narrows her eyes. "What?"

"I got fully invested in Luna, for what? For him to say we can't actually protect her?"

The door to church swings open and Axel fills the doorway. "What the fuck are you bitching about, VP?" he barks.

"You scrapped my idea?" Lexi asked, sounding hurt. "So, what, you were just doing it to keep me quiet?"

"Of course not, Mouse. He's just pissed I won't let him go on a rampage."

"You're a prick, yah know that?" she spits, storming off.

"Great, thanks for that," he growls, shoving me hard. "Throwing me under the bus won't make me give in. You stay the fuck away from Nate, am I clear?" I stare at him, anger radiating from me. "Are we fucking clear, VP?" he roars.

"Yes, Pres," I spit, storming off.

LUNA

I wake with a start to find Grizz standing over me. I scoot away, confused by his angry glare, and he immediately steps back, showing me he isn't here to hurt me. "What are you doing in here?" he asks.

I look around, remembering I snuck into my old room, the one I shared with Ivy, while he was in church. I must have fallen asleep. I push to sit up and realise I'm still clutching Ivy's blanket. "It smells of her," I whisper, staring at it. "I just needed to smell her."

He gives a stiff nod and takes a seat in the rocking chair. "We need to talk about what happens next."

"Okay."

"I don't want you alone with Ivy at all."

My heart breaks some more. "I'm her mother, Grizz. I've been raising her alone all this time."

"And a fine job you did of that," he mutters, rubbing at his forehead. "I just can't work out why you didn't tell me."

"So, now, you're going to punish me and keep me away from my daughter."

He fixes his angry eyes on me. "*Our* daughter, and you didn't seem to mind keeping me away."

"Only I didn't, did I? You were in her life."

"But not as her fucking dad," he yells. "I'm not punishing you, Luna. I'm keeping Ivy safe."

"You heard Becki, she said I can be alone with her for short periods. I'm not a risk to my own daughter," I cry, tears of frustration falling.

"And she also said Ivy is being put into my care. So, while she's in my care, I get to make the decisions. You're not to be alone with her. You'll work in The Bar for me and get your life together. And then I want you out of here."

My heart twists. "I'm getting her back," I whisper. "This isn't a permanent thing."

He sneers. "You really believe that, don't you? Your life is a fucking mess. Just look at your mum and the support you don't have. You'll end up just like her."

I get up from the bed. "You're wrong," I mutter, leaving the room.

I head downstairs and straight for the bar. "Whiskey," I mutter, taking a seat. Smoke pours me half a tumbler, and I take it gratefully, drinking half down and wincing as it burns my throat.

"Careful there. That stuff's the real shit, not that watered-down crap you get in bars nowadays." Cooper sits beside me and orders the same. I drink the rest and hold up my glass for a top-up. Grizz's words are swimming in my head, and I can't help but think he's right. The self-doubt is too strong to ignore.

"Yah know," Coop adds, sipping his own drink, "whatever it is, you won't find it at the bottom of a bottle."

I sigh heavily. "You sure, Coop? How do you know?"

"Cos I've been there," he tells me. "And I've also witnessed it. Drinking your problems away won't get you the end result."

"It's not the drink that'll stop me seeing my baby girl, it's Grizz."

"And you're just gonna let him?" he asks, swirling his drink around in the glass.

"He'll fight me. I can't afford lawyers and court costs. She's already been removed from my care—the courts will side with him over me."

He sits back in his chair. "I would've given anything for Widow to fight for Lexi. I was in a similar situation to you and Grizz, and I trusted her to fix up and take care of our daughter. After I left, she just got worse. I came back and took Lexi, and she didn't even put up a fight. It was like she was glad to see the back of us."

"I don't want to leave Ivy," I say, more tears falling. "It's not my choice."

"But it is," he says, gently placing a finger under my chin and turning me to face him. "You're a queen, Luna, and you need to straighten that crown and fix up. Prove to Grizz that you're a good mum. Don't let one mistake define how this will go. Because if you do, you're gonna wake up twenty years from now and realise you've repeated history. Break the cycle, Luna. Fight for what you want." He finishes his drink and stands. "I know you're a good mum cos I saw it with my own eyes. Fight for your daughter so she knows, even if you don't win, you at least tried."

I stare into my glass as Lexi fills the vacated seat. "That looked serious," she says, staring after her dad. "Are you okay?"

I shake my head. "Not really."

"Me either. Axel is a complete knobhead. What's Grizz done?"

"Do you hate Widow?" I ask.

The question surprises her and she frowns. "I don't hate her, but I don't love her either."

"Would you change it, your upbringing and past?"

She smiles, shaking her head. "No. Widow never put me first. Dad always did. He left this life for me so he could raise me safely. Widow couldn't even put down a drink to feed me. But if it hadn't been for my history, I wouldn't have made it back to the club and I wouldn't have found Axel again. So, in some ways, I'm grateful she was my mum, but not for the reasons I should be . . . if that makes sense."

"Grizz doesn't want me in Ivy's life."

"He said that?"

I shake my head. "Not exactly, but it's what his end goal is. He doesn't want me to be left alone with her. He's giving me a job at The Bar, and when I get back on my feet, he wants me to leave."

"Without Ivy?"

I nod. "He said I'll end up like my mum."

She scoffs. "I didn't."

"But you got away. I've been in this life so long, I'm not sure how to get out. I tried . . . God knows I tried, but no one wants to employ a prostitute. I have zero experience in anything but lying on my back."

"That's not true," she says. "You're a businesswoman." I laugh at her words. "You handle money, you book in clients . . . take those skills and apply it to something else. You make bread, right?" I nod. "Then get a loan and start up a bread-making business."

I give a defeated laugh. "That's way out of my league. Besides, who would offer me a loan?"

She shrugs. "I don't know, but there must be some scheme

out there to help you. I'll look into it. In the meantime, prove to Grizz that you're not giving up. That's what I would've wanted my mum to do, to fight for me."

I head back upstairs, grab a notepad, and begin coming up with ideas. If I can work out some figures, maybe Lex is right—maybe I can follow my dreams and prove Grizz wrong.

I'm so lost in numbers, I don't notice Grizz standing in my doorway sometime later. I glance up when he clears his throat. Cali is hanging off his arm, and I ignore the ache it causes. She gives me a sympathetic look before telling him she'll wait in her room for him.

"I shouldn't have been so harsh back there," he says, but his face isn't giving me apology vibes.

"No problem."

"But even you have to see there's some truth to it. Ivy needs stability. She needs a parent who'll put her first."

I tap the pen on my chin. "How much do you think a food van would be?"

He frowns at my random question. "What?"

"Yah know, a food van, like with an oven and stuff."

"Why?"

I pick up my phone and tap it into a search engine. "I'm over it," I mutter, flicking through the pictures of used vans. "And for the record, I gave Ivy stability in the beginning, I just got a little off track."

"She got put into care," he says bluntly.

"She did," I say, nodding, then I look up at him. "I messed up. That won't happen again."

"Sure," he says, rolling his eyes.

"And if you think I won't bring up your past in court—and the fact you're quite happy to fuck prostitutes, hence how Ivy came to be—you're mistaken. Because I might suck cock for a living, Grizz, but I spent many years being silent while the men around me talked. I know so much about you and your past, it's enough to put you back inside."

He closes the gap between us, his face full of rage. "Are you threatening me?"

I nod. "Yeah, I think I am."

"You have no idea what I can do to you."

I smirk. "I think we just established I do know. And for the record, stick your fucking job up your arse."

CHAPTER 15

GRIZZ

I don't bother to find Cali. My hard-on disappeared the second Luna made that threat. After everything I've done for her, she repays me with threats. *Fucking bitch.* I snatch the bottle of whiskey from behind the bar.

"I just had Luna sitting here doing the exact same thing," says Coop. "You're both so angry, you think the bottle will solve it."

I slam it down. "Makes sense she's drunk," I snap, "seeing as she just threatened me."

"Oh, yeah, with what?"

"My past, like that'll get her Ivy. Doesn't she realise a judge will end up putting the kid in care permanently?"

"The way I see it," he says, taking the bottle from me, "she's fighting for her daughter."

I narrow my eyes. "What did you say to her?"

"I told her the truth, that she's a good mum and she should fight for what she wants."

"So, you're the reason she's up there coming up with crazy ideas about food vans?"

"Don't you think that little girl needs her mum?"

"I think she needs someone who won't let her down," I snap.

"When I look at Luna, yah know what I see? A product of her environment. She loves Ivy, and up until recently, she was a good mum, working hard to provide as a single parent."

"She didn't have to do that. I was right fucking here," I argue.

"No, but she chose to do that. Have you even asked her why she'd bring a baby into this world and choose to do it alone rather than tell you? And have you thought about what happened in her life to have her go from being a good mum to having her child taken into care?"

Her hurt expression at seeing me with Danii filters into my mind and I shut it down. "Her kid should always come first, no matter what. You took Lexi from Widow for the same reason."

"I loved Widow," he tells me. "I didn't care about her past. I only left when it was clear she was so hard into drugs and drink that she couldn't give them up for us. I thought leaving would make her see what she'd lost. All it did was put Lex at risk. And when I took her, it was the hardest thing I ever did. I prayed Widow would get her shit together and come back for our baby, cos Lex needed her mother in her life, but when she didn't, it about broke me all over again.

"I didn't take Lexi to spite her or to teach her a lesson. I wanted them to have a relationship, but Widow didn't feel the same way. Luna is different. Up until you came into her life again, she was doing good. And all I see right now is a heart-broken, vulnerable woman who messed up. I told her she's a queen. I told her she's a damn fine mother. I told her the things you should've told her when she came to you for help.

You have the chance to help her so that you can both be good parents to that little girl. Don't blow it."

———

It's almost eleven in the morning when the social worker finally brings Ivy home. Luna sweeps her into her arms and takes her over to the couch, where she buries her face into our daughter's soft body, whispering how much she's missed her.

Becki gives me a reassuring arm rub as I watch them together. "It's good she's got you to support her," she tells me.

Once she's gone, I take a seat beside Luna, who eyes me cautiously, probably waiting for my next blow. Instead, I smile. "It's good to have her back."

"She doesn't smell right," Luna mutters, unfastening the baby grow. "She needs a bath and some fresh clothes."

"Would you mind if I did it?" I ask.

"What, now you don't trust me to bathe my own daughter?" she snaps.

"Actually, I'd like to spend some time with her now I know the truth."

She rolls her eyes and hands Ivy over without a fuss. She follows me upstairs and hovers in the doorway while I set up the baby bath. When I go to undress her, she steps farther into the room and closes the door before popping her elbow into the warm water to check the temperature. "It's safer to check with your elbow," she tells me. "Your hands aren't sensitive to hot water."

I give a nod. "Okay."

"And this one smells nicer," she says, grabbing one of the three bottles of wash I'd bought especially for children. "It's got lavender and it settles her." She then places the towel on the radiator. "I always wrap her in a warm towel after her bath," she mutters, shrugging.

"Do you remember your mum ever doing any of this sort of stuff for you?" I ask, slowly lowering Ivy into the water, holding her exactly how Luna taught me to just a few weeks ago. "Not when you were a baby, obviously, but as you got a little older?"

Luna sits on the closed toilet. "No. Never. Do you?"

I shake my head. "I don't really remember my parents."

"Mum wasn't always so bad. There were times when she did things like make us sandwiches or even cook a hot meal. But they were few and far between. When I think about growing up, I remember shouting and doors slamming. I remember her crying a lot."

"Ivy deserves better, right?"

"And I'll give that to her."

I resist the urge to roll my eyes. "You turned down my job. So, how?"

"I've got a plan. I'm going to make it work."

"You have a plan with no money, no home. Ivy will have a large family here at the club, and she'll never be short of people who will look out for her."

"I know what you're doing," she mutters, "and it makes me feel like I'm not good enough. But I am, Grizz."

"That's not what I'm saying."

"Why did you choose her?"

I glance back at her. "Who?"

"Danii."

I groan. "Don't start."

"I'm not," she says, "I swear. It's a genuine question. Why did you choose her over me?"

I lift Ivy from the bath, and Luna rushes to grab the towel, helping as I wrap Ivy and hold her to me, inhaling her lavender baby smell. Luna was right, it smells good. "Because . . . because you remind me of my mum."

"Right, and the minute you saw I had Ivy, you said a

similar thing. You had no faith in me from the start. You knew I'd fail and you were just waiting."

"That's not true," I snap, heading into the bedroom. I lay Ivy on the bed and begin to dry her.

"If I had a good job, if I was never a club whore, and you met me, would you choose me or her?"

"I'm not answering that."

"Because you know I'm right. I was never going to be good enough for you. You were always going to fight against me. That's why I couldn't tell you about Ivy."

LUNA

I have no intention of arguing on Ivy's first day home, but I can't help feeling angry at Grizz for comparing me to his mum.

He lets me feed Ivy and then I leave him to put her down for her nap. I have a plan to put into action if I'm ever going to prove him wrong.

I grab a cab over to the bar where I know I'll find Reaper. It's been a while since I've been near the Kings, and as I enter, it doesn't bring back any good memories. Reaper stands when he spots me, leaning down to kiss my cheek. "You're looking good, mama," he comments, pulling a seat out for me to sit.

"Thanks for agreeing to meet me."

"How could I not? You know I have a soft spot for you."

I blush. "I'll get straight to the point. I'd like to borrow money."

He frowns. "What for? Cos if it's for your brother, no. I've washed my hands of him and I told your old man he was welcome to him now his debt's been paid."

It's my turn to look confused. "Nate paid off his debt?"

Reaper leans back in his seat, smirking. "You should talk to your old man, Luna."

"I don't have an old man," I say firmly. "Did Grizz pay off the debt?"

He moves to stand, like he's going to leave, and I rush to grab his hand. He stares down at where my tiny hand touches his and lowers back into his seat. "I don't need no trouble with the Demons, baby girl. Grizz came in here to tell me he was saving you from your brother, and honestly, it's about time someone did. If I'd have known how bad things were, I'd have done it."

I release him and place my hands in my lap. "The money isn't for Nate. It's for me."

"Does Grizz know you're here?"

I shake my head. "No. We're not a thing. He hasn't claimed me. I need a better life for me and Ivy."

"How much are we talking?"

"Twenty-five grand."

His eyebrows arch in surprise. "Fuck, that's quite a sum."

"I'll pay every penny back."

"How? Luna, that's a lot of money, and as far as I know, your only source of income was Zen, which apparently you're no longer working at."

"I'm buying a pizza van."

He rests his arms on the table and fixes me with a serious look. "You want to borrow twenty-five grand to purchase a pizza van . . . why?"

"So I can make bread."

He throws his head back, laughing loudly. "Just when I think I can't be surprised," he says, wiping the tears from his eyes. "Jesus, Luna, that's a sentence I never thought I'd hear you say."

"Can you help me or not?" I ask, my tone brisk. I am so over men doubting me.

He gives a shake of his head and my heart sinks. "Look, I'd love to come along on the crazy bread van idea, but my money is tied up. And I'll be honest, I don't need Grizz on my back."

"He doesn't need to know."

"Oh, he does, Lu, he really does. Have you thought about applying for a government scheme or going to ask the bank?"

I shrug. "A bank won't lend me a penny. Forget it, I'll come up with something."

"If you need a job, I can sort that," he says.

I stand. "No offence, but those days are behind me."

He smiles. "I meant in the bar pulling pints."

I lean down to kiss him on the cheek, and his hand slips in mine. "I would've saved you, yah know. You and Ivy. You just had to ask."

"I know," I whisper, gently running my free hand over his cheek. "But it wouldn't have been fair to you."

"I take it Grizz is the father." I give a nod. "I always wondered why you wouldn't stay away from that club."

———

I decide to pop over to Mum's seeing as I'm in the area. I've only been gone half an hour, so I'm sure Grizz hasn't noticed I've left the clubhouse yet. I need her to know how angry I am for everything she's done to me, and then I'm walking away. For good.

When I step inside, the first thing I notice is how clean everything looks. The hall carpet has been hoovered and is no longer littered with cigarette ash, crumbs, and other debris. I frown, glancing into the kitchen as I pass and seeing it's spotless.

I find Mum sitting in the living room, staring into space. "Mum?" She jumps in fright, but when she sees it's me, she dives up and throws her arms around me. I'm so shocked, I don't respond. "I've been so worried," she cries. "I had no idea how to get in contact with you. How's Ivy?"

I bristle at her words, stepping from her arms. "That's why I'm here."

"Oh shit, don't tell me they've taken her into care, Lu." I shake my head, and she sags in relief.

"She came home today."

"Oh my god, I've been so stressed."

"You have no idea what the last few days have been like for me," I say, rolling my eyes. "In fact, you have no idea how you've fucked my life up."

She lowers into her seat and buries her face in her hands. "I do. I know I've messed up over and over."

"Messed up?" I repeat, scoffing. "You ruined my life, Mum. Thanks to you, I've lost my daughter."

She looks up. "But you said—"

"Grizz is making my life very difficult. He's treating me like I'm a risk to my own kid, and I don't know if he'll fight me for permanent custody. All I wanted to do was be a good mum to her, and you fucked it up for me."

"If I could change it, I would. Nate said he was doing it because he cared."

"So, he did call social services on me?" I ask, even though I'd guessed as much.

"I sent him away, Luna. I told him not to come back." Nate has always been the favourite child, but I could never work out if it was because she was terrified of him or she just preferred him over me. "I realised if I didn't get him out of our lives, he'd make sure you ended up exactly like me."

I groan, rubbing my hands over my face. "I already am, Mum, don't you see it? I've been living your life since I was eleven years old." When I look at her, I notice silent tears rolling down her cheeks. "Why did you make me do that stuff?"

"We needed the money," she whispers.

"Bullshit. I need money, but it doesn't mean I'd ever sell my daughter to strangers."

"I haven't always made the right decisions," she admits.

I laugh, and it's cold and empty. "Tell me one good decision you made."

"Having you," she says, swiping her tears away.

"No," I yell, "that was the worst decision you ever made. You brought me into this world and made my life hell. You were supposed to protect me."

"Nate said the same," she mutters, staring at the ground. "He was so angry."

"You weren't fit to have kids. I would've been better off in care than with you."

"You see, Nate wouldn't leave," she continues as if I haven't spoken. "He just kept yelling at me and then . . . and then he . . . he was going to hurt me," she says, finally raising her gaze to me. "And I saw it in his eyes, that same look men get when they're too lost. He was high and drunk, and I think he would have . . . maybe he didn't know it was me. Maybe he was so lost, he didn't see I was his mother." I'm frozen to the spot, listening to her rambling. "And I didn't know what to do. He was so close, and I was terrified. It was one hit . . . maybe two. And he just went down." She begins to cry.

"What are you talking about?"

She glances past me towards the bedroom door. "I didn't know what to do and I couldn't find you."

"Did you call an ambulance? Is he in hospital?"

She shakes her head, her eyes still fixed past me. My heart slams hard in my chest as I turn towards the bedroom door. I move towards it, then rest my hand on the doorknob, too terrified to turn it in case Nate comes charging out in anger. I take a deep breath and turn the knob until it clicks. I glance back at Mum, who is staring wide-eyed at me.

The second I push the door, a smell hits me like nothing I've ever smelt before and I instantly gag. Covering my nose and mouth with my jumper sleeve, I push the door until Nate's feet come into view. I wince, stepping in. Nate's still body is on the bed, looking up at the ceiling. His eyes are open and there's blood soaking the sheets around his head.

I quickly close the door and rush out of the flat, gasping in fresh air to replace the scent of rotting flesh. I'm shaking so hard, my legs feel like they'll give way. Mum steps out and whispers, "What shall I do?"

I stare at her blankly. "Why didn't you call an ambulance?"

"He was already dead."

"So fucking what?" I hiss, glancing around to make sure no one's listening. "It was self-defence, right?"

She nods. "But I panicked. What if they didn't believe me?"

"They're not going to believe you now. How long has he been here?"

"The same night they took Ivy." I take a few steps back away from her, and she frowns. "You can't leave me," she hisses.

"Are you mad? I can't sort this, Mum. I've got Ivy to think of."

That cruel look returns and I brace myself for the blow. "If you don't help me, I'll tell them it was you."

"They wouldn't believe you. I've got an alibi."

She smirks. "You don't think Grizz would use it to get you out the way? I'll tell the police you came back and attacked us, and then you locked me in the flat with no way to call for help."

"You're fucking deluded," I mutter.

"Are you willing to risk it? Grizz will get Ivy, and you'll go to prison."

I run at her, slapping her before she can escape back into

the flat. "You fucking evil witch," I scream, shoving her to the floor.

The neighbour pops his head out the window to see what all the commotion is. "Help me," Mum yells. "She's lost her mind."

Panic takes over and I release her. "It's nothing, a family argument," I tell him, holding out my hand for Mum to take. She does, smirking as I pull her to her feet. "Nothing to worry about."

He looks at Mum for confirmation, and she nods. "I'll be fine."

We go back into the flat. "I fucking hate you," I hiss, pulling out my mobile.

Axel answers on the second ring. "Luna, where the fuck are you? Grizz is losing his mind."

"What are the chances of me getting your help without you telling Grizz?"

He laughs. "Zero, baby. What have you done now?"

CHAPTER 16

GRIZZ

Luna answers the door looking sheepish. My hand grips her throat, forcing her up against the wall. "First, you sneak out to ask another man for money, and then, you ask my President to keep shit from me?"

"You already hate me, Grizz, I didn't need this thrown at me too," she mutters.

I release her as Axel walks past and goes into the living room. "What's going on?" he demands as we follow him.

"Mum killed Nate," says Luna, and we both share a surprised look. "And she's threatened to tell the police it was me if I don't help her."

I glare at Luna's mum, who doesn't look the slightest bit embarrassed by any of it. "You're a piece of work," I mutter in disgust.

She grins. "Take a good look, lover boy, because in a few years' time, she'll be exactly like me. Like mother, like daughter."

"Where is he?" asks Axel.

Luna points to another door, and Axel goes to check it out. "Jesus," he mutters as the stench of death fills the living room. "How long's he been here?"

"A couple days," says Luna. "She's had the heat on, which is fucking amazing seeing as she never usually puts it on."

"Go back to the club. Scooter is waiting in the car park for you," I tell Luna. "We'll talk when I get back."

"What about me?" her mum asks.

"You can rot in hell," snaps Luna. "From this day on, you're dead to me." And then she leaves.

"Ungrateful bitch," her mum mutters.

I go into the bedroom where Axel is wrapping the body in the blood-soaked sheet. "What do we do about the witch?" I ask.

Axel sighs. "She can't live. She's the type to put this on us, or worse, on Luna. I'll send someone to sort it later. I'm thinking a cigarette in bed to start a fire. That way, we'll burn this mattress and it'll look like an accident."

"I'll do it," I say. "Clean up won't come to fetch Nate until dark. I'll stick around till then and slip something in her drink to make her sleep."

Axel grabs a pot of pills from the bedside table and shakes them. "Sleeping pills prescribed in her name."

I take them and stuff the bottle in my pocket. "It's just one thing after another with her," I mutter, and I feel his eyes on me. "Luna," I add for clarification.

"At this point, you may as well marry her," he says, smirking. I narrow my eyes, and his smile fades. "You've already done more than any brother has for a club girl. It screams love."

"In case you haven't noticed, I've not had much choice in any of this. And now, she's the mother of my kid. I can't see her going to prison, can I? Especially for something she didn't even do."

"What do you think she wanted the money from Reaper for?" he asks.

I shrug. "But if it's anything else that's gonna lead to trouble, she's gone."

"Gone?"

I give a nod. "When a club whore asks for cash and goes to the trouble of approaching another club, it's got to be drugs or something else illegal. No whore ever did good with that amount of cash."

"Whore," he repeats, arching a brow. "Interesting choice of words."

"It's what she is, no?"

He gives a small, unamused laugh. "I think you're doing it to push her away, to distance how you really feel about her. It's easier to refer to her as something you hate, then maybe you'll believe it."

I roll my eyes. "Next, you'll be telling me she's a changed woman."

"Even I can see she's trying, brother. She wants to be better than this," he mutters, looking around the messy bedroom. "And she wants to be a good mum."

"And if she gives me the right answers, she might just get the chance to," I say, winking before leaving the room.

There's an uncomfortable silence that stretches between me and Luna's mum. I don't have the energy to entertain this fucked-up bitch. She's smoked at least ten cigarettes, one after another, and every time I catch her eye, she looks away quickly, like she might die from making contact.

I sigh heavily and light my own cigarette. "So, what happened?" I ask, nodding at the closed bedroom door.

"I know you judge me," she spits, "but it's not easy, yah know, bringing up two kids on my own with no fucking money."

"I ain't asking for your life story," I mutter, inhaling on the cigarette before slowly releasing the smoke. "I wanna know what made you kill that fucker before I managed to."

She smirks. "So, you're not pissed I killed him, just that I beat you to it?"

"I had a score to settle."

"And you think I didn't? He might have been my son, but he was far from a good person."

"Yeah, Luna told me all about him," I say, bitterness lacing my tone.

She scoffs. "She thinks she's had such a hard life. She'll have you believing she was a victim in all this."

"Wasn't she?"

"She was a promiscuous girl right from very young, always flirting with the men and fluttering those long eyelashes they all loved. And she didn't speak—they loved that shy bullshit she gave off. Sweet, innocent, cute, and she had the looks to go with it." She says the words through gritted teeth, like she's jealous. "One night, I came home late, and you know what she was doing? Fucking her dad's best friend while he watched. She was eleven."

Sickness stirs in the pit of my stomach. "What?"

"Exactly. Eleven years old and trying to please grown men. He never looked at me the same again after that," she mutters, staring off into space. "I could see it in his eyes—he wanted her, not me."

I wince as she spits the words in anger. "You think that was her fault?" I ask, crushing my cigarette in the overflowing ashtray.

"She wanted attention. Her dad brought his friends back and they all loved her over me. And then he was gone," she clicks her fingers, "and we were left with his debts. And the men didn't stop coming. They'd had a taste of her and were lining up, so I had no choice but to charge. How the fuck else would I have fed and clothed her?"

"She was just a kid," I mutter, scrubbing my hands over my face.

"Mature for her age," she says.

"But still just a kid," I repeat. "All that shit should've been hidden from her. The drugs, the drink, the sex."

"She was always clinging to me," she snaps. "How the hell was I meant to work with a kid clinging to my side?"

"She was probably fucking terrified," I suddenly yell, and she jumps in fright. I stand, releasing a long breath to try and keep calm cos as much as I want to end this fucking bitch, I can't. Not yet, and not with my hands. "You made her think she didn't have a choice. You and Nate sold her for your own gains."

"I knew she'd tell you some sob story," she scoffs. "Why else would you want her?"

I turn to her, pushing my face to hers until she's practically lying back in the chair, her eyes wide with fear. "Being forced into prostitution by the woman who's meant to protect you isn't a fucking sob story," I growl. "You make me sick."

I move away and grab the half-drunk whiskey bottle from the side. I go to the kitchen and grab two glasses. Pulling out the pill bottle, I empty the contents into the glass. I'm surprised when I find a rolling pin in a drawer, arching my brow as I shake my head. I can't imagine her baking.

I use the end to crush the tablets into a fine powder then spoon some into the other glass and half fill it with the amber liquid. I give it a stir, waiting for the powder to disappear before taking the bottle off the side and carrying that and the glass back into the living room. I hold the glass to her, and she eyes it suspiciously. When she makes no move to take it, I roll my eyes and sit down on the couch. "Fine, I'll drink alone." I move the glass to my lips, and before I'm forced to take a sip, she holds out her hand for it.

I give it over and take a swig from the bottle. "My mum was like you," I say. "A whore who justified it by saying she had to put food on the table somehow."

"Being a parent is hard. You'll see."

I scoff, taking another drink. "She'd say that too. I used to look at other kids' mums in the playground at drop-off and think, why doesn't my mum smile like the others? Why was her life so fucking hard and the others seemed to have this easy life?" I drink again. "And yah know what I realised when I grew up? She made it harder than it needed to be. She could've just worked in a supermarket or a takeout shop. Selling pizza would've put food on the table. There were other ways, and she wouldn't have been so sad about it, but she chose to neglect me and fill her body with drink and drugs. She thought they were worth more than her own son."

"It's not easy," she mutters. "You think it is, but for a single mum, back then, it was hard."

"And what about now?" I snap. "Did you never think once to sort your shit out and be a mum, a grandmother even?"

She rolls her eyes then knocks back her drink and slams the glass on the table. "She'll only fuck that kid's life up—"

"Like mother, like daughter, eh?" I mutter.

"Exactly."

I snatch the glass up and head back to the kitchen. I gave her enough to make her drowsy, but I'll need the rest to make her sleep soundly, so I top the glass up a second time and stir in the tablets. Then I clean the rolling pin and the glass I used to crush the powder up. I wipe the worktop then take the drink back into the living room, where Luna's mum now looks a little sleepier. She squints at me, blinking a few times. "You might think I'm a crap mum—"

"Because you are," I cut in, handing her the glass. This time, she takes it without staring at me accusingly and drinks a large mouthful.

"But I taught her everything she knows," she slurs.

"That's not something to be proud of."

She narrows her eyes, drinking back the rest of the glass. She swallows then frowns and looks into the glass, seeing the remnants of powder. "What have you done?" she hisses.

"It's time for you to sleep," I say, taking the glass and placing it on the table.

"Jesus, I don't give out freebies," she snaps, fighting me off when I try to grab her wrist.

"And I don't fuck whores," I mutter, getting a firm grip and hauling her to her feet.

"You fucked Luna," she says, giggling and almost falling back into the chair. I swoop down and scoop her into my arms. "Call her. We can do a two-for-one deal."

"Jesus," I mutter, shaking my head in disgust.

"Who doesn't love a mother-daughter duo?" she demands, laughing again while running her hand over my cheek. "In another life, you'd have been my type," she adds thoughtfully. I kick the bedroom door open and dump her on the bed beside Nate's body. "We can't fuck here," she gasps.

"We ain't fucking," I snap, shoving her back so she's lying down. She blinks a few times. "I really tried," she whispers to no one in particular, "to be a good mum. I wanted to love them, I just didn't know how." Her eyes drift closed. "I'm sorry," she mumbles. I wait a few minutes before prodding her arm. She doesn't respond, and I sigh in relief.

There's a knock at the door and I go to it, pulling it open

slightly to find the clean-up team. "Am I pleased to see you," I say, letting them in.

Once Nate's body is gone, I move Luna's mum into a half-sitting position. I place one of her cigarettes between her lips and light it, watching as it slowly burns, occasionally dropping the ash down her front. When it's halfway down, I place it between her fingers and rest her hand beside her. I take the empty bottle of tablets and give it a wipe before placing it on its side on the floor.

I wait patiently for the sheet to catch fire. It burns quickly, catching the curtain beside the bed as well as the mattress beneath it. I step from the bedroom, closing the door behind me and wiping the handle with a towel I took from the kitchen. I straighten the cushions where I sat then go back to the kitchen and clean the glass she used. I dry them and put them away, and when I return to the living room, smoke is beginning to come under the bedroom door. It's my cue to leave, so I head out, dropping the latch on the door.

LUNA

I jump in fright, opening my eyes and staring up into Grizz's. His hand is over my mouth and he smells of whiskey. "Why are you in my bed?" he asks, then he removes his hand so I can answer. I lean up on my elbows and look around the bedroom he once said was mine.

"I wanted to be closer to Ivy," I admit. I insisted Duchess let me put Ivy to bed, even though she watched my every move.

"I left Duchess in charge."

"She was here," I tell him. "I must have fallen asleep."

He goes over to the Moses basket to check on Ivy, who is sound asleep. His eyes are full of love whenever he looks at her, and it warms my heart that she's got a father who will do anything for her. "I'm sorry I called you to sort out Nate," I mutter, dragging my knees to my chest and resting my chin there.

"Only you didn't call me," he says, not bothering to look at me.

"It was just another thing," I say. "I didn't want to be more of a problem."

"I never said you were a problem," he snaps, this time turning to me. "You went to Reaper?" he adds, moving closer. I can see the anger burning in his eyes.

"You stink of smoke," I mutter.

"Being in that shit pit with your mother for hours has gotten into my clothes," he snaps and begins to strip. He keeps hold of his kutte but places the rest in a bin bag. "So, Reaper?"

I stare at the ground. He's completely naked now, and I'm not sure where to look. "I wanted a loan," I say, shrugging.

"I know. He said. What for?"

"That's my business."

I see his feet as he steps closer. "You'll give me answers now or you're out of here."

"Out?" I ask, bringing my eyes to his. "You'll kick me out?"

"You're here because I allow you to be. My patience is running out, Luna. What did you want twenty-five grand for?"

I stand, and he steps back. "I wanted to open my own bread van."

He frowns. "Bread van?"

"I saw it on social media. A guy got a food van and made bread, selling it on the move. It works."

He looks surprised. "You want to start a business?"

I fold my arms over my chest. "I really think you should put some clothes on," I utter.

He gives a stiff nod. "Don't go anywhere." He leans over to lock the door, as if to ensure I stay put, so I drop back onto the bed while he heads for the bathroom. "I just need to shower."

When he returns, there's a towel wrapped around his waist. "From the beginning," he says, grabbing another towel to rub his wet hair.

"I've seen a van and I needed the cash to buy it."

"Why Reaper and not me?"

"He doesn't judge," I admit, shrugging.

"You think I judge?" he asks, sounding hurt.

"You compared me to your mum," I remind him. "Look, I want to have a better life for Ivy. And I was doing fine until you came along." He tries to speak, but I hold my hand up to stop him. He presses his lips together in a firm line, so I continue. "I know that making money by selling myself isn't conventional. I never wanted to do that, but it was a trap I got into. When Ivy came along, I vowed to make enough to sort myself out and then I'd get a decent job. But you came along and . . . well, you made me think I was worthy to have a better life."

He sits opposite me. "You are worthy."

"And then you dropped me, and I was right back there, to the times my parents would sneer at me and call me useless. I doubted everything, even my ability to be a mum to her," I whisper, looking over to Ivy. "My heart broke, Grizz, and I took too long putting it back together. I let the doubt creep right in until it took hold and ripped me apart. But losing Ivy has woken me up, and I know you don't think I'm good enough for her, but I am. I am a fucking good mum. I love her so much and I'll do anything to protect her, so I'm going to stand on my own two feet and get what I want."

A small smile pulls at the edges of his mouth and his hand cups my cheek. For a second, I think he's going to kiss me, but he doesn't. He just stares. Eventually, his thumb brushes the corner of my mouth. "I was wrong—"

"No," I say, pressing a finger to his lips. "Don't say it. Not until I've proven you wrong."

A small laugh escapes him and he nips the pad of my finger. "Fine. How are we going to get you a business?"

I shrug, remembering I didn't get the cash I needed from Reaper and he was my only hope. "No idea, but you're not giving it to me, otherwise, I won't be able to prove you wrong."

"How about you work for me?"

I begin to shake my head, and he places his other hand on my cheek and holds me still. "Don't kiss me," I mutter, my eyes pleading.

His frown softens and he gives a slight nod. "I spoke to your mum tonight. She told me some stuff . . . about your dad and his friends." I pull free from his hands and put some space between us. If he didn't judge me before, he certainly will now. "Luna, it wasn't your fault."

"It's why he left," I say quietly, avoiding his eye, "because I disgusted him."

"No, it wasn't. In fact, I think the alternative is so much worse. It wasn't because you disgusted him, Luna, it was because he wanted you and couldn't have you. He knew it was wrong."

I shudder, pulling my knees to my chest again. "My mum said it was my fault he left us, and that I had a responsibility to bring in money."

"She's an evil woman, Luna. And I know you're not like her. I know you're a better mum than she ever was." I glance up and see the sincerity in his stare. "I was wrong, and I used your insecurities to push you away so I wouldn't fall for you. I fucked up."

"You really hurt me, Grizz," I admit. "I can't hurt like that again. I've been used by men my entire life and I can't do it anymore."

Hurt passes over his face, but he gives a slight nod. "Make bread in the bar. I have a food license, so you can save up what you earn and buy a van or whatever you want."

I stare down at my lap, twisting my fingers together. "It's a great offer," I mutter.

"I don't expect anything from you, Luna. Make bread. It's amazing and it's a crime not to share it with the world. When you have a plan and the money you need, I'll let you go with no questions. You're Ivy's mum, and she deserves to see how amazing you are."

"I don't know, Grizz. Things just get messy when we're together."

"You wanna prove me wrong, right?" he asks, and I nod. "Then take the offer. You're not inundated with them."

I sigh. He's right. It's the only offer I'm likely to get, and it's just temporary. "Okay. We'll give it a go."

CHAPTER 17

GRIZZ

I stand in the doorway of the bar and watch Luna as she stares in awe at the brand-new kitchen. I'd had it built at the rear of the bar just in case we decided to do snacks. "It's small, not big enough to knock up a three-course meal, but just—"

"Right to knock up bread," she finishes the sentence, turning to face me with a huge smile on her face.

I press my mouth to Ivy's chubby cheek. "I think Mummy likes it," I whisper.

"I love it, Grizz, and I swear I won't let you down."

"This is about you and your dreams," I remind her. "You're not letting me down whatever happens."

"But you didn't have to do this," she says, her voice low. "I appreciate it."

I check my watch. "Well, everything you asked for is in the cupboards. Rugby starts in five hours and we've got at least twenty hungry guys coming in expecting beer and bread."

She moves closer, gently leaning in to kiss Ivy, before looking me in the eyes. "Thank you."

I hand Ivy over to Dutchess and head into church. Axel's already begun without me, filling in the men about Luna's family issues and how we dealt with them. "You don't deserve her," says Coop on a sigh. "Poor girl."

I roll my eyes. "I'm trying to make shit up to her," I argue. "I got her making bread to fulfil her dreams."

Duchess bursts in. "Sorry, Pres, but the police are just pulling up outside."

"Did they say what they wanted at the gate?" asks Axel, standing. She shakes her head, and he glances my way before following her out.

We all file out just as he's letting them into the clubhouse. He calls me over, and I join him. "They're looking for Luna," he tells me, acting surprised.

"She's at work," I say. It's no secret the police aren't welcome in the club, and they look just as uncomfortable as we feel. "I can pass on a message."

The female officer shakes her head. "We really need to talk to her. It's important."

"I'll take you to her. She's just around the corner."

We walk in silence. I haven't told Luna about her mum, and she hasn't asked, not for details at least. It was for this moment, and I'm hoping to God she doesn't blow it.

The second I open the door to the bar, we're hit with the smell of fresh bread. I smile, unable to control it. From the kitchen, her sweet singing fills the air. I stop in the doorway right as she turns to face me mid-song. She stops dead, a blush creeping over her cheeks. "Oh shit, you scared me."

I grin. "Sorry, but you've got visitors." I move towards her and turn as the police enter.

Placing an arm around Luna's waist, I gently pinch her side to snap her out of the terrified expression she's currently hosting. She clears her throat. "Is everything okay?"

"Luna Carter?" the officer asks, and Lu nods. "I'm afraid we have some bad news," begins the female officer. "There was a fire at your mother's property last night."

Luna gasps. "Is she okay?"

The officer gives a slight shake of the head. "There was nothing they could do to save her. We think she may have fallen asleep with a lit cigarette."

Luna slams her hands over her mouth and her eyes fill with tears. "Oh shit. She's dead?"

"We're so sorry for your loss."

"The neighbour told us about your brother, Nathaniel," the other officer says.

Luna's head snaps up, and I pull her into my side a little harder. "What about him?" I ask.

"We were wondering where he is. The neighbour gave us his number, and we were trying to get hold of him last night to tell him the news. He said Nathaniel was next of kin being the oldest?"

"Luna has nothing to do with him," I snap. "He's a twat."

"I can try and get hold of him," says Luna quietly, "but I doubt he'll answer me. I'll probably have to leave a message."

"The neighbour said Nathaniel lived with your mother. We checked the flat and there was no sign of him. The fire was contained to the bedroom."

"He was always in and out of her life. He's into drugs," Luna explains. "He was her pimp."

The officers raise their eyebrows. "So, you can see why Luna has nothing to do with him," I say.

"Again, we're sorry for your loss. If you have any questions, the coroner has the body." The officer hands a card over with a telephone number on it. "They'll contact you when the body is released for the funeral."

I show them out, and when I return, Luna is kneading dough. "You stopped singing," I point out, leaning in the doorway.

"A fire," she whispers, bringing her eyes to mine. "Was she awake?" I give my head a shake. "I want to hate her," she eventually adds, "but it's hard. Harder than I thought it would be."

"She didn't suffer," I say, "and it wasn't a choice, Luna. She was a risk to us all. She would've held that over us and tried to put the blame on either you or the club. We couldn't risk it."

She nods, keeping her eyes fixed on the dough. "I know, just it would've been nice to have a heads up."

I move closer and place my hands over hers, stilling them. "They needed to see an honest reaction, Lu. But you did great back there."

"It's why you smelled of smoke," she murmurs, her eyes filling with tears. "And it's another thing you did for me." A tear escapes down her cheek, and I catch it on the pad of my thumb, brushing it over her soft skin.

"I keep messing shit up, Luna. I was looking at you all wrong. I'd do anything for you and Ivy. Anything at all."

"I'm not ready for anything," she whispers.

"I know," I reassure her. "And even if you were, I don't deserve you. Not until I've made things right between us."

"After everything you've done," she says, a sob catching in her throat, "I owe you so much."

"No," I say firmly. "I didn't do any of this for favours, Lu. You don't owe me. I treated you like crap and then tried to make you feel like you weren't good enough. But you are.

You're more than." I place a gentle kiss on her forehead. "We'll take it slow."

LUNA

When Grizz suggested beer and bread, I didn't think it would work, but I was so wrong. We're already a month into the trial, and the customers are coming in especially for the bread. The smell drags people in from the street, and we're always packed out on the three nights we offer it.

I place the last loaf to cool and wipe my hands on the towel. "Are you ready?" I glance up to find Grizz in the doorway. He looks handsome in a black suit, even without his kutte.

I give a nod and inhale a deep breath before releasing it slowly. "Ready than I'll ever be."

He holds out a hand, and I take it. Nothing's happened between us apart from a few fleeting moments where he's almost kissed me but never quite executed it. We've even survived shared parenting with Ivy, and although she still sleeps in Grizz's room, he hasn't made me feel pushed out.

We drive in silence to the church. It's only ten minutes up the road, but I'm wearing heels and I didn't fancy the walk. When I met the vicar to discuss my mum's funeral last week, I opted for no fuss and a late cremation.

When I step from the car, it's almost dusk. I fold my arms over my chest and stare up at the beautiful building. "You okay?" asks Grizz, coming to my side and placing an arm around my shoulders. I give a slight nod, and we proceed to the church.

It's cold inside. I chose not to have flowers as this funeral is already costing a fortune, and quite honestly, I don't think she deserved flowers. But now, as I look around the church, it seems empty without them.

The cardboard coffin is placed at the front and the vicar rushes up the aisle to greet me. We shake hands, and he does the same with Grizz. "Shall we start?" he asks.

I take a seat in the front pew, and Grizz slides in beside me. The vicar takes his place at the front and clears his throat, just as the church doors open. I turn, watching as Axel and Lexi step inside, followed by London, Duchess, Verity, and all the other club girls. A smile pulls at my lips when the rest of The Chaos Demons file inside, all filling the pews behind me. Lexi places a hand on my shoulder. "We didn't want you to do this alone," she whispers. "We're your family."

Tears spring to my eyes, and she hands me a tissue. I take it, laughing as a sob slips out, then I turn to Grizz, who's watching me closely. He does that a lot. "Thank you," I whisper, leaning my head against his shoulder, because I know he organised this for me.

The service is over quickly. I chose a short poem and opted not to say any words. What is there left to say? I wait for the coffin to be taken into the furnace before I turn to leave, followed by my new family.

Outside, Smoke is rocking Ivy in the pushchair. I smile, going over to rescue him. "Thank you so much," I tell him, looking in to check she's wrapped up warm.

"I'll take her back to the clubhouse," says Duchess, and I begin to protest but Grizz steps in, nodding and thanking her.

Then he takes my hand. "We'll catch everyone up at the club. I just want to do something first," he says, leading me away from everyone.

We go back to the car and drive in silence for ten minutes. He stops at a restaurant and rushes round to open my car door. I frown as I step out. "What's going on?"

"It's been a tough day. We can't just pretend it didn't happen, so we're having dinner."

My frown deepens. "This place looks fancy," I remark as he closes the car door and grabs my hand.

"It's the best."

I slow as we get to the door, reluctant to go inside. He stops and turns to me. "What's wrong?"

"I've never done this," I say, shrugging. "I don't know how."

He grins. "You don't know how to eat?"

"Of course, I do. I mean, I don't know how to act in a place like this."

His smile softens as he brushes his thumb over my cheek. "Me either, so let's do it together."

Inside, it's posh. The sound of cutlery tapping plates and gentle conversation sends fear through me as a waiter shows us to a table. A few people look up at Grizz, his size making him stand out.

My seat is pulled out and I slide into it, feeling my cheeks burn with embarrassment. Grizz sits opposite me. "Guess I stand out even without the kutte."

"They're probably wondering what I'm doing in here," I whisper, taking a menu from the waiter and opening it to hide behind.

Grizz takes it from me and lays it down flat. "You're no different than these people," he says firmly. "In fact, you're better."

I scoff. "I doubt that."

"Luna, you're better than anyone in this damn room, including me."

"You don't have to do this, yah know."

His eyes narrow. "What?"

"This," I hiss, waving my hand around the room. "A fancy dinner."

"I wanted you to see you're special."

"Why?"

"Because I owe you so much. This is just one small thing in a long line of ways I'm going to make it right between us."

"Things are fine," I say. I look around the room, taking in the expensive décor. I feel so out of my depth.

I feel Grizz take my hand in his. "Don't look at them, look at me," he says gently, and I do. "Stop comparing yourself."

"It's hard not to," I mutter.

"You're beautiful," he says, smiling.

I blush, even though he says those words to me every day. "What sort of food do we order in a place like this?" I ask, turning my attention to the menu.

"Steak, obviously," he tells me, signalling for the waiter to return and placing our orders. "Two glasses of water as well," he adds, giving me a knowing smile.

Since Mum died, I haven't touched a drop of alcohol. I'm not sure if knowing she and Nate are both gone makes me feel at ease, or if I just got tired of the same routine, but I looked at Ivy that night and decided from that day on, I was never going to drink again. I have no need too. I'm not hiding anymore.

"You can drink," I tell him.

"I want to keep a clear head," he says, "cos we need to talk."

Dread fills me. He's brought me here to soften the blow he's about to deliver, because whenever anyone sits me down to talk, it's never for anything good.

"Just hit me with it quick," I say, retracting my hand.

He frowns. "Relax."

I take a breath. "Okay, I'm ready."

He smiles, and it confuses me. I've been waiting for him to tell me to leave the clubhouse. The social workers have been happy with Ivy's care and are on the verge of helping us put together a parenting plan so we can share access. The thought of moving out of the clubhouse breaks my heart because it means not having full access to our daughter. "Why do you always assume the worst?"

I fiddle with my napkin, avoiding his eyes. "Because good things never happen to me."

He grabs my hand again. "Look at me, Luna." I don't, and he gives my hand a gentle squeeze. "Please."

I raise my eyes, and he's smiling. "It's not bad. In fact, it's a business proposition."

"Oh?" It's not what I was expecting.

"I'll be honest, I didn't think the bread thing would work in The Bar, but you know yourself that business is booming and I think that's down to your hard work." I blush under his praise. "I want to make it permanent."

I gasp. "Really?"

"I know you had ideas about setting up on your own, and if that's what you want, I get it. But I like how we work things, and my profits are through the roof right now, so I'd like you to stay."

"Wow," I whisper, a million thoughts racing through my mind. "I mean, it's a great idea. I love working there—"

"You don't work for me," he reminds me. "You run that kitchen, you keep the profits. This is your business and that should become official."

"What do you mean?"

"Set it up in your name. A business name. Pay your taxes, rent the space, whatever it takes to make your own name because I know that's important to you."

"I don't even know how to do any of that," I mutter.

"Cash will help with your books. He'll help you set up everything."

"My own business?" I repeat, a smile forming.

"You'll be able to support Ivy properly, do all the things you want."

"Are you sure?" I ask. "You've already done so much for me."

"Lu, I'm serious when I say this is a business opportunity for me too. I'm bringing this to you as a businessman, not a friend."

His clear friend-zone makes me sit a little straighter. I love him, there's no denying it, and even though he's hurt me more than I've ever been hurt before, I can't help my heart wanting him. But he's right—I've worked hard to make the bread become a good part of his business, even creating flavours to suit certain beers. I'm good at what I do and I know I can make a business work.

I smile. "I'll be a businesswoman," I say, and he grins.

"Is that a yes?"

I nod, and he leans over the table, kissing me on the cheek. "Amazing." I feel disappointed it's just on the cheek, even though I've been keeping him at arm's length. He's been so kind lately, it's hard to remember why I'm guarding my heart from him.

CHAPTER 18

GRIZZ

She looks so happy, and it makes my heart swell. I want so badly to kiss her, I've felt the need more than once and had to restrain myself. She's not ready, and I have to respect that, especially after the way I've treated her.

By the time we get back to the clubhouse, Duchess has laid out a few sandwiches and cakes, and everyone is gathered in the bar for the wake. I know Luna didn't want a fuss—her mum certainly didn't deserve one—but this is about Lu and making sure she knows we're all here for her. The second we walk in, she's enveloped in hugs from the women. I step away, allowing them space, and head over to where Axel sits with Coop.

"She good?" Axel asks.

I give a nod, unable to keep my eyes off her. "She's agreed to stay at The Bar."

"Thank fuck," he says, slapping me on the back. "Business is booming."

"So, why do you look so fucking cut-up?" Coop asks.

I shrug. "I'm happy she'll be around longer."

"But you want her to wear your kutte and stick around for you rather than The Bar?" he guesses.

I sit on the stool between them, still watching Luna as she speaks with London and Lexi. "I fucked up so much, she's never gonna forgive me."

"She will," Coop reassures me. "Just keep showing her your support and it'll flow naturally."

"I don't deserve it, Coop. I'll never be good enough for her."

"You're damn right there," he agrees, smirking. "But you'll get her anyway cos pricks like you always come out on top." He nudges his shoulder against mine in jest. "Seriously, VP, she's gonna come around. Just give her time."

I see the wary look on Luna's face and I know she's exhausted. So, I head over and rescue her from Lexi, grabbing her hand and hauling her to her feet. "Bed," I order.

"Yours or hers?" teases Lexi.

"Oh, we're not . . . it's not like that," says Luna, blushing.

"But Grizz wishes it was," adds London, winking.

"We're friends," says Luna, glancing at me for backup.

I don't bother to reply. Her friend-zoning me in front of the women only cements what I thought—she's still not ready.

I lead her upstairs, but instead of going up to her room, I head towards the room I've been sleeping in with Ivy. The room she used to occupy before I was a complete prick. "What's going on?" she asks as I push the door open and gently guide her inside. I linger in the doorway, still holding onto her hand.

"You should be in here with her," I whisper so as not to wake Ivy. "This is your room, yours and Ivy's."

She frowns. "I thought I wasn't allow—"

"I've been a dickhead, Lu. I've been so consumed with anger." I sigh, dropping her hand. "You're a good mum, and you've always been a good mum. I was letting my past control my head. You're nothing like my mum."

She stares down at the ground. "Now I'm earning a living the way you think I should," she mutters. She raises her head and her eyes are full of hurt. "Being a good mum is providing for your child. I was always doing that, just not in a way you accepted."

I give a nod. "I was out of order."

"And I know I messed up. I hold my hands up. But it wasn't because I was a bad mum. It was because I was trying too hard to be good. Sometimes we get it wrong, and I got it wrong, but I always tried, and in my opinion, parenting is fifty percent practise and fifty percent failure. She didn't come with a handbook, and I totally wing it every day, but so do other parents, not just the ones who work in unconventional jobs. I want to forgive you, Grizz, but I'm not sure I can. And I don't know how I feel about this sudden turnaround because you're finally not ashamed to be seen with me."

"I was never ashamed," I argue.

"You didn't look at me then the way you look at me now. I still had sex with all those people," she says, and I look away. "That will never change. And the words you said to Axel, about you not being able to get past that, is what's holding us back. I can't change my past. I will always be that club whore, and worst of all, I'll never forget what you said about me."

"How do I make it right again?" I ask, my tone pleading. "Because I can't imagine not making this better so we can be together." There's a look of finality on her face and it scares the shit outta me. A lump forms in my throat. It's never happened before, and I swallow it down in a desperate attempt to not show my emotion. "Please, Lu. Don't tell me this is it, that we're not going to make it."

Ivy stirs, and she turns to look in that direction. "I missed out weeks of her life," she whispers, "because you said I wasn't good enough. What changed?" She stares at me for a long minute, and when I don't respond, she closes the door gently.

I lean my forehead against it and squeeze my eyes closed. I don't remember the last time I cried, probably not since I was a little kid, but right now, the urge is strong.

I head to my own room and grab my gym bag. It's the next best thing to necking a bottle of whiskey.

LUNA

"You said what?" gasps Lexi, staring at me in disbelief while I knead some dough. Having filled her in on last night's exchange between me and Grizz, I expected to feel better, but with the way she's looking at me, I'm not so sure.

"I did the right thing, right?" She raises her brows and nods, even though she doesn't look convinced. "Lex, come on," I say with a groan. "You were the one who said I needed to be honest about how I felt."

She nods again. "You're right, I know. And you needed to be honest, but damn, girl, that must have cut him deep."

"He looked tortured, Lexi. Absolutely broken. And I haven't seen him at all this morning. He didn't even come in to kiss Ivy."

"He was in the office with Axel when I left to come here," she tells me. "The conversation looked deep."

"Have I made a mistake?" I ask, putting the dough in the proofing tin.

"No . . . no." She sighs. "But this isn't the end . . . is it?" I glare at her, and she holds her hands up. "Okay, sorry. It's just, yah know, he's done a lot of good things too."

"And I'm grateful."

"He covered up a murder," she whispers, "and got rid of that awful woman from your life."

"You're not helping here," I snap.

"And when he bought Ivy all that stuff for her room," she says, smiling and clutching her hands to her heart, "it was so sweet. And he didn't even know he was her dad at that point."

I brace myself against the worktop and hang my head. "I fucked up, didn't I?"

"Maybe you could've left a little wiggle room for forgiveness," she says, shrugging. "He seems to realise how much he messed up."

"I should talk to him," I mutter, my heart squeezing in my chest. I can't get that gutted look he had on his face from my mind. It tortured me the entire night.

"Perhaps just tell him you're still open to exploring a relationship."

The bar door rings out, and I glance through the kitchen to see Grizz. "You have to go," I whisper to Lexi, and she grabs her things.

"Good luck," she whispers, air-kissing me and rushing out.

Grizz looks up in surprise as she passes him. "Where's the fire?" he asks, dumping his books on the bar.

"She remembered she had things to do," I say, leaning in the doorway. "You okay?"

He nods. "Yeah, great. You?"

I shrug. "I guess. Look, about last night—"

He's already holding his hand up and shaking his head. "Forget it. I have." I clamp my lips closed. "You're right. Let's just concentrate on Ivy. We got this co-parent thing working now and we don't wanna mess things up again."

"We don't? I mean, we don't."

"Great, so we're on the same page?" I give a nod, and he grins. "I'm hiring a bar manager today," he says, changing the subject, "so you won't have to see my face all day." He laughs, but I don't join him. I look forward to spending time here with him, away from the club.

"Oh."

"Did you speak to him?" whispers Lexi when I finally get back to the clubhouse.

I flop down beside her on the couch and shake my head. My feet ache from being on them all day and I feel miserable inside. "He's had time to think and he agreed with me. He wants to concentrate on Ivy and working out co-parenting." I cover my face with my hands and groan. "What if he wants me to move out?"

"He wouldn't. He loves having you and Ivy here."

"He might insist on keeping Ivy here. And what happens when he finds an old lady? She won't want me here."

"You're overthinking."

"I'm being realistic. I've blown it."

"Luna Carter, unless he's got an old lady, it's not over. So, don't give up. Go and tell him you miss him."

"Miss who?" asks Fletch. "Me?" He wiggles his eyebrows, and I smile as he sits beside me.

"God, no," I joke.

"She thinks she's blown things with the VP," Lexi says, and I elbow her. The last thing I need is Fletch running to tell Grizz.

Fletch grins wider and places his arm around my shoulders. "You want me to help?"

"No," I say right as Lexi says yes.

Fletch looks around the room. "He's already zoned in on us," he says with a smirk. "He's got it bad for you."

"I doubt that," I scoff. "We decided to be friends earlier... or co-parents, at least." Fletch laughs and moves to the table in front of us, perching on the edge. He slides his hand down my leg slowly, and I frown. "What are you doing?" Then he lifts it so my foot is in his lap.

"Showing you it's not done."

He pulls off my shoe and presses his thumb against the arch of my foot. My head drops back in pleasure. I should tell him to stop, but his hands feel so good right now as he massages the ache away. "Oh, Christ," I murmur. "Where did you learn to do that?"

"Baby, I feel bad if you've never had a foot rub before," says Fletch, working his thumbs along my heel.

"Uh-oh," he mutters, "angry VP incoming." He presses against the arch again, and I cry out in delight.

I feel Grizz's shadow fall over us. "What the fuck's going on?"

"Did you know she's never had a foot rub?" asks Lexi.

"Two seconds," Grizz hisses, "and then I'm breaking your fingers."

Fletch releases my foot, and I groan in protest. "Just trying to help the lady out, VP."

"Make it the last time your hands touch her like that," Grizz warns, and Fletch stands, giving me a wink before sauntering off.

Grizz takes his place and lifts my foot into his lap. "That was harsh," I say, closing my eyes again as he begins to rub my foot.

"Yeah," agrees Lexi. "He offered to rub her back next."

I give her a warning side-glance as Grizz's grip tightens. "You better be fucking joking."

"She is," I say quickly. "Relax."

"You realise she won't be single forever," Lexi continues. "You can't threaten every man who comes near her. You don't own her."

"Pres," yells Grizz, and Axel comes over. "Remove your old lady from my presence."

Axel smirks. "What are you doing now, Mouse?"

"I'm reminding Grizz that he doesn't own Luna."

"She's winding you up," I tell Grizz. "Keep rubbing," I add. He swaps my foot, and I moan in delight.

"Come on, Mouse, let's go practise massaging . . . upstairs."

Lexi jumps at the chance and rushes off to follow Axel. "They're like rabbits," I murmur, suddenly feeling relaxed.

"Duchess is feeding Ivy. You want me to run you a bath?"

I open one eye. "Sure." I'm not going to pass up the opportunity to get a relaxing soak. He places my foot on the floor and holds out a hand for me to take.

Upstairs, he goes to the bathroom to run the bath as I sit awkwardly on the bed. He's never done this sort of thing and it feels weird. "I can . . . erm . . . massage your back."

I feel a blush creeping up my cheeks. "Lexi was kidding. Fletch never offered—"

"I'm offering," he cuts in, pushing his hands in his pockets. "Yah know, in case you need one." He frowns like he's working out his next words. "But if you think it's weird or—"

"No," I say a little too quickly. "No, I'd like that."

He gives a nod, going back into the bathroom to turn the tap off. When he comes back, he's holding a bottle. "Oil," he mutters in explanation.

"I've never . . . had a back massage," I admit.

"You gotta take that off," he says, pointing in the general direction of my shirt.

I give a nod, standing to lift it over my head. I turn away, keeping my back to him, and then I crawl onto the bed, lying face down.

It's a few seconds before he moves towards me. The bed dips as he throws a leg over me, straddling my thighs. "You mind if I unfasten the bra?"

"Sure," I whisper.

He unclips my bra and slides the straps down my arms. He drips oil onto my back and the coldness breaks me out in goosebumps. "I can't believe no one's ever done this for you," he says, his voice sounding sad.

His hands run up the centre of my back, and I gasp at the contact. He glides them over my skin, sending electrical pulses through my entire body. "Oh wow," I mumble, "that feels so good."

Grizz works his magic for another twenty minutes, easing the muscles in my back until I feel like a new woman. When he climbs from me, there's no hiding his huge erection. He grins, shrugging before going back into the bathroom to finish the bath.

"It's ready," he shouts a few minutes later.

I stand, holding my bra in place and going into the bathroom. I close the door behind me, and he eyes it warily.

"I've never had a bath with anyone before," I tell him as I drop my bra to the floor. "I thought you could be my first for that too."

He inhales sharply, his brows arching in surprise. I push my jeans down my legs, followed by my underwear. I daren't look at him in case I see horror on his face, so I go ahead and get in the bath. Sliding into the water, I immerse my hair and then sit up and move forward. I hear him undress, but I keep my eyes fixed forward until he climbs in behind me and pulls me against him.

I lie on his chest, and he wraps an arm around me. "Thank

you," he whispers against my hair. "For asking me to be your first."

CHAPTER 19

GRIZZ

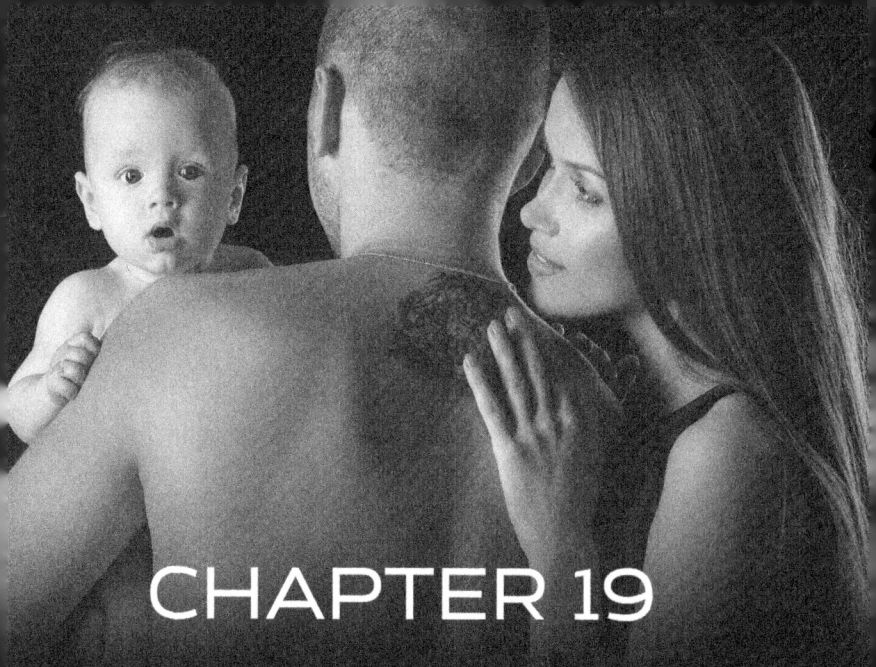

We sit in silence for some time. I don't want to presume this means something, even if deep down, I think it does. Seeing Fletch sniffing around Luna again was a reminder of how much I've thrown away, but being here with her now gives me hope.

"There are other firsts," she says, gently running her fingers over my knee. "As well as the dinner date."

"Yeah?" She nods, and I take the sponge and load it with her favourite bodywash. "Like?"

"We've never been parents before."

"True." I run the sponge over her shoulders, and she sits to lean forward so I have access to her back.

"I didn't give them everything," she whispers, and I pause the sponge, watching the suds drip down her skin. "I had sex with men, but they didn't get everything. They didn't see me bake . . . they never heard me sing." My heart twists for her and the shit she's been put through. I pull her to lie back against me and run the sponge over her chest, squeezing the soapy water over her breasts. "I never kissed them."

"You didn't?"

She shakes her head, twisting slightly so she's looking up at me. "Only you."

I move my mouth closer, and she inhales, waiting for me to close the gap. "And from this point on," I murmur, "it will only ever be me." I kiss her. It's slow and meaningful, and I pour my feelings into the kiss, praying she understands what this means.

When we finally break apart, she's panting with need. "And I've never made love."

I groan. "I'm trying to take it slow here," I whisper.

She turns, facing me. "And I've never been in a relationship." She's looking right into my eyes, waiting for me to say something. Instead, I pull her to sit over me and kiss her again. My erection presses at her entrance, and when she slides onto me, I let my head fall back and watch as she gently moves, taking her time to ensure the water doesn't spill over the edge.

"You're giving me all your firsts," I say, running my hands up her body and cupping the back of her head to pull her back in for another kiss. "No more excuses. I'm yours."

She pulls back, gripping the edge of the bath as she moves faster, letting her orgasm control her. "No more," she pants in agreement. "I'm yours. Completely yours."

Gripping her waist, I still her, even though it pains me. "I mean it, Luna. This is it. There's no going back." She gives a nod, her breaths coming out as shallow pants. "Don't agree to it if you're not all in," I add, and for the first time in my adult life, I feel vulnerable. I want this so badly, I'm terrified she's just agreeing in the heat of the moment.

She leans closer, wrapping her arms around my neck. She looks me in the eyes. "I am in love with you, Warren." I inhale sharply. No one's used my name in such a long time, unless you count the prison guards or the police. "I have been in love with you for so long, I don't even know when I first realised, but it was before Ivy and before you ever noticed me. So, I am one hundred percent certain that I am completely yours . . . forever."

A peace washes over me as I hold her against me, pushing to stand with her in my arms. "No one will ever touch you again," I murmur in her ear as I carry her through to the bedroom and lay her on the bed.

I kiss her, trailing my lips down her neck and body, parting her legs and swiping my tongue against her swollen clit. She bucks off the bed, running her fingers through my hair. "All mine," I mutter.

And she is. Now and forever. Always mine. I won't let her go. We belong together, and I will spend eternity showing her how fucking amazing she is.

LUNA

"Man, I can't tattoo her without the bra gone," says Ink, sounding exasperated.

I've been in the chair for ten minutes now waiting for Grizz to relax. I want the tattoo of his name on my side, right next to my breast. "He's not going to see anything," I argue, turning onto my side and lifting my arm. "You can make sure of it," I add, smirking.

Grizz huffs, sliding his large hand into my bra and covering my breast. "Fine. Make it quick."

Ink unclips my bra from the back, moving it enough to give him access to my skin. I close my eyes when the needle buzzes to life. There's something about the gentle scratching of the needle that I love. Grizz squeezes my breast and cocks a brow. "You like the pain, Lu?" he asks.

It's been a crazy few months since we decided to give things a go, but I don't regret a single second. Grizz is everything I need him to be and more. He's an amazing dad to Ivy and the perfect man for me. And I love being his old lady. I finally feel like I belong somewhere.

"All done," says Ink, sounding relieved. He covers the tattoo and then turns away so I can sit up and replace my bra.

Grizz gets in the chair, and before I can move away, he grabs me and lifts me to sit over him. I smile, wrapping my arms around his neck and laying against him. Whenever I'm within grabbing distance, he wraps himself around me.

Ink shakes his head in annoyance and begins to draw on the small space on Grizz's arm. I stare at my name on his skin and smile. "I like it," I say, kissing him.

Ink makes vomit noises before turning away to replace the needle. I rub against Grizz, feeling his erection swell beneath me. "You're a bad girl," he whispers, nipping my neck.

Ink returns, firing the gun up for a second time and setting to work. When he's finished my name, Grizz pushes me to sit up and Ink moves closer. I watch as he free hands Ivy's name on Grizz's chest.

The second the gun stops, I kiss him. "Get out of here," he tells Ink, only pulling away for a second to get the message across.

"Seriously, VP, I've got another booking in ten minutes."

"I'll take five," Grizz pants, already unfastening his jeans. I laugh as Ink stomps out the shop. "You heard the man, we've got five minutes," he growls, lifting my skirt to my waist and moving my knickers to one side.

I sink onto him. "You know, if we keep having spontaneous sex," I say, digging my fingers into his shoulders as he fills me up, "we'll end up with a lot more Ivys'." I think that's his plan, but I haven't voiced my suspicions until now.

He thrusts his hips faster. "Fuck, Lu, talking like that's gonna make me come."

I giggle, bracing my hands on his chest. "You like the thought of me pregnant?"

He shudders hard, coming. "Jesus," he pants, reaching between us to finish me off. I come seconds later, then he tugs me to his chest and kisses the top of my head. "I wanna keep filling you with babies," he pants.

"I'd like that," I admit. "I want to share it all with you this time."

"You realise I'll be an overbearing prick," he says as I slide from him and straighten my clothes.

"More than you already are?" I tease, stepping back before he can grab hold of me again. But secretly, I don't mind. I love how he watches my every move, and how whenever a man is near me, he's ready to pounce, even when it's innocent, like in the supermarket line.

And he's my first. My first love. My first best friend. My first real kiss. My first family. But my last relationship.

Because no matter what, he'll always be my life. Him and Ivy.

It took us too long to get here, but now we are, I'll never give it up. I'll never give him up.

THE END

About the Author

Nicola Jane, a native of Nottinghamshire, England, has always harboured a deep passion for literature. From her formative years, she found solace and excitement within the pages of books, often allowing her imagination to roam freely. As a teenager, she would weave her own narratives through short stories, a practice that ignited her creative spirit.

After a hiatus, Nicola returned to writing as a means to liberate the stories swirling within her mind. It wasn't until approximately five years ago that she summoned the courage to share her work with the world. Since then, Nicola has dedicated herself tirelessly to crafting poignant, drama-infused romance tales. Her stories are imbued with a sense of realism, tackling challenging themes with a deft touch.

Outside of her literary pursuits, Nicola finds joy in the company of her husband and two teenage children. They share moments of laughter and bonding that enrich her life beyond the realm of words.

Nicola Jane has many books from motorcycle romance to mafia romance, all can be found on Amazon and in Kindle Unlimited.

Other Books By This Author

<u>The Kings Reapers MC</u>

Riggs' Ruin

Capturing Cree

Wrapped in Chains

Saving Blu

Riggs' Saviour

Taming Blade

Misleading Lake

Surviving Storm

Ravens Place

Playing Vinn

<u>The Perished Riders MC</u>

Maverick

Scar

Grim

Ghost

Dice

Arthur

Albert

The Hammers MC

(Splintered Hearts Series)

Cooper

Kain

Tanner

The Chaos Demons

Axel

Grizz

Fletch (Coming Soon)

Follow me on social media.

I love to hear from my readers and if you'd like to get in touch, you can find me here . . .
My Facebook Page
My Facebook Readers Group
Bookbub
Instagram
Goodreads
Amazon
I'm also on TikTok

Printed in Great Britain
by Amazon